SAWYER'S REGRET

A Contest with Circumstances

E. Raymond Tatten

D1522622

ALSO BY E. RAYMOND TATTEN

AND ANOTHER THING just saying...
2018

TEX MOSTLY
2020

MOVING WILLIE
2020

SAWYER'S REGRET

DEDICATION

To the memory of Ms. Claire Endicott Sears whose
contributions inspired an awareness in myself and others of
New England's indigenous peoples. Ms. Sears's
accomplishments include the creation of Fruitland's Museum's
"Indian Museum" in Harvard Massachusetts and her published
account, *The Great Powwow* that chronicles portions of the
history of the people who inhabited the Nashua Valley before
the Europeans arrived.

For all sad words of tongue and pen,
the saddest are these,
"It might have been."

John Greenleaf Whittier

One hundred years before the American Revolution, cultures clashed in Colonial America with mistrust and treachery culminating in a contest that left over one-third of the "New England" colonial population slaughtered along with thousands of Native Americans.

Thirty years later, the next generation continued the deadly struggle.

This story was inspired by true events.

ONE

I T WAS OCTOBER 15, 1705, in the settlement of Lancaster on the frontier of the Massachusetts Bay Colony. Sixteen-year-old Elias Sawyer leaned against rough fireplace stones, balancing to slip on his second boot before he set another log to freshen the morning fire. He felt the warmth surround his legs as he tugged on a linen jacket before easing through the dark room, moving as quietly as possible so as not to wake the others. Seven families with thirty-seven souls were crammed into his family's two-story, wooden garrison house. Even though King Philip's War had been over for thirty years, surprise Indian attacks had continued for years, and no family would be foolish enough to ignore the mandate to sleep in a fortified garrison.

Elias's father had risen earlier in the dark to feed the pigs. When he returned, he and Elias began the walk to their family sawmill, passing stone foundations and remains of homes burned years ago by Phillip's raiders, along with houses still abandoned until the Indian threat was gone for good. The Wampanoag people had been either killed or driven away, but deadly raids from Canada continued. Only the most determined settlers like the Sawyers were brave enough to return for another try.

As they walked, Elias shuffled his feet, rustling through a crisp, shin-high covering of dead autumn leaves. The predawn fall air stung his face, cold until the sun would rise above the horizon. With first light, a portrait of oak, maple and elm trees would blaze color: oranges and reds on the maples, crimson-walnuts and chestnuts along with bright yellow poplars. Bone-white birch trees, the first to lose their leaves, were already almost bare.

They arrived soon at the wooden enclosure that straddled Dean's Brook, dammed to create a pond and squeeze a controlled spill that spun the twenty-foot wooden waterwheel alongside. An attached pole moved the gear inside the small structure, turning the sawblade most of the day, ripping logs as fast as neighbors' oxen could drop them. In Lancaster, flat boards were a most valuable commodity; the Sawyers were successful, and Elias was learning the trade. At sixteen, he was ready to prove himself.

It was a perfect work-morning — cool inside but not yet the biting cold a New England winter would bring. The thick smell of sawdust from freshly cut pine logs hung in the air. Teeth of the steel sawblade reflected flickering candlelight, and although still dark, it was almost time to snuff the candle. Elias and his father leaned their most important possessions, flintlock muskets, in the corner against the wall before considering the first work. Since the morning air was moist with heavy dew, they had kept their weapons cased for protection. In Lancaster, fathers taught sons to keep a musket close, often the difference between life and death. The advice to "keep your powder dry," was not just a suggestion.

But careful preparation and caution were never enough when an enemy used the oldest proven tactic — the advantage of surprise.

TWO

M R. SAWYER MOVED near the sawblade with familiar instructions Elias often heard to begin each day's work.

"Pull that first log and let me know when you're ready. Then I'll start…"

The words stopped with a muffle and a pained grunt that startled Elias. He turned to see dark shapes, figures of men wrestling in the shadows. His first thought was his musket, but he had been careless, leaving the weapon on the other side of the room — unready. He lunged toward the corner, but after two steps, silent attackers appeared as if evil spirits from the afterlife, surrounding him before he could get far.

Two men tackled Elias, slamming his head against the rough, oak floor, pressing his face on its side. While he fought to stop wetting himself, a rawhide noose tightened around his neck, cutting off his breath. His mind raced. *Is this what it feels like to die!* His arms were yanked behind him, and he heard the grunts from the others' fighting. With one eye, he saw his father slashing with his musket. A scream rocked the room as Mr. Sawyer crashed his gun against one man's arm, then drove the next swing into the neck of another before the men closed around him. He fumbled to fire, but it was too late. Attackers swallowed him with a flurry of punches.

They grappled, one man striking Mr. Sawyer on the side of his head before another brandished a long knife close to his eye. The Indian muttered strange, angry-sounding words then flicked the blade against Thomas's cheek, opening a gash that released a stream of bright red blood. Elias tried to cry out, but his voice was muffled when a rough hand stuffed a rag into his mouth. Sharp pain rocketed from the middle of his back when a man's foot rammed his body flat. His hands were bound, the skin on his wrists stinging from the pinch of rawhide rope. He was hauled to his feet and held near his father who stood with bleeding face and bloodied nose, his shirt-front red. But Elias saw no fear, only his father's calm.

All that mattered was to survive. One of the captors yanked the rawhide line, pulling Elias outside. Trotting to keep up, he saw about twenty in the raiding party that stretched thirty yards in front and behind. Although the sun's first rays had not broken over the horizon, the pink glow was enough. The attackers wore deerskin britches, some with bare chests and rawhide bands across their upper arms. Their faces were smooth, some painted with black stripes. Each brave's head was shaved on one side with a tuft of hair on top, long enough to fall along the neck. Feathers flapped from headbands.

They were all breathing hard when the line reached the blackness under the trees on the edge of the Sawyers' rye field where they met a few others. With no resting, the swollen war party moved again, snaking along the trail beside the brook that spilled from the mill pond. Since the land sloped down, the running might have been easier, but Elias's feet already stung. His lungs burned. With his hands bound, he found moving difficult, but he had to keep the line slack and keep up with the others. Any time he lagged or lost his balance, he was jerked by the rawhide, the noose already beginning to break the skin on his neck.

They followed the river, with the only sound the noisy current splashing past rocks as it dropped from the northwest. Elias glimpsed his father and another white man as the line ahead slid downhill closer to the riverbank and a flatter trail. The stranger was younger than his father, maybe thirty-five like one of Elias's uncles. He was attached to the Indian directly in front by a rawhide line, his hands lashed together in front.

Elias's stiff leather boots were not made for running; he prayed the attackers would stop to rest, even for a few minutes. All he could think about was the pain throbbing in his hands, feet and neck. *If only they would stop running. Please, God, make them stop…*

They climbed with the rise of terrain, swallowed inside the dense vegetation. The leader stopped the group inside a border of low brush that edged the thicker woods. With the sun higher in the morning sky, the day felt hot as the men crouched and listened, out of sight of anyone who might be following.

The captives were pushed to the ground before a large brave approached from the front of the line, kneeling first next to the white stranger, then next to Mr. Sawyer and finally Elias, checking the noose and the knot on his hands. When the warrior looked satisfied, he grunted a command, and the war party moved again.

Elias dreaded each next step. Sharp pain stabbed from each heel — first when he picked up his foot, and again when he stepped. There were blisters, and he was sure they were bleeding. If he could get a boot off, he might never get it on again.

They trotted uninterrupted until the late day sun touched the western treetops. When the war party stopped to gather where a brook met the river, the leader stepped closer, surprising Elias.

"You, English! Drink!"

A young warrior holding Elias's leash led him close to the brook. When Elias knelt near the water's edge, he pitched forward into the water before managing to right himself. Then he knelt and gulped until the burning in his throat quieted. When his thirst was finally satisfied, he dunked his head before struggling to his feet, cold water splashing inside his shirt and down his chest and back. When he turned, he found his father surrounded by three men, his face swollen and bloodied. He must be thirsty too, but the devils had not offered him water.

"Come on!" Elias snapped, addressing the leader and gesturing with his head toward his father. "My father drinks too!"

The big man studied Elias, looking at Mr. Sawyer, and then back to Elias. There was animosity in the air as Elias waited, unsure of the leader's reaction.

"Father drink!" Elias repeated, with more emphasis.

The leader approached Elias as if measuring him with no hint of emotion. A wide scar creased one of his muscular upper arms. His face was marked with a black design under each eye; a beaded, tan band circled his thick neck. Elias had never been close to an Indian and had never seen what looked like hate in a man's eyes. The stern man stood with hands on hips before he turned to the braves surrounding Elias's father. With strange-sounding words, he barked at the guards who tugged Mr. Sawyer to the edge of the water where he waded into the stream and knelt to drink. Then the other white man was also led to drink. When they were all satisfied and still standing close, the stranger began to speak.

"I'm John Bigelow — from Marlborough. They…" An Indian stopped him with angry-sounding words and a strike on the back of John's head. When the leader was satisfied, he gestured, and they moved again, trotting in silence along the edge of the river that twisted with the contour of the land. With no verbal communication and no more resting, the men shuffled through the night and into the morning as their caravan snaked through the trees, continuing north along the western riverbank. The water level was low with places to cross, the water only hip-deep and moving slowly. Elias and his grandfather had hunted deer nearby, and the familiar river provided some comfort, almost like a friend who had been with them on the trail. But today was different. He was a captive, fighting fear and fatigue, wondering if he could survive. *Where were the others? When was an alarm sounded? Were their friends chasing? Please God*, he muttered, *show them our trail!* His neighbors and uncles, Peter and Abraham Sawyer, would be chasing, but the blanket of leaves hid their tracks making it almost impossible to follow. Since rescuers could only guess the kidnappers' trail, friends must have guessed wrong.

Elias had considered himself strong, but now he was beyond fatigue — just about done in, dragged with the last of his strength. As the Indians maintained a steady trot, Elias began to come to grips with his situation. His shoulders hurt, his hands and heels stung, and he was worrying more about keeping up. *What will happen if I cannot go on? Where were they taking us? Are they going to kill us?*

He had thought his captors might have headed for Wachusett Mountain on the western horizon. His grandfather said there had been Indian camps there in the past, and it was a likely destination. But they were heading north. *How much longer could these men keep this pace?* Elias realized, if you are running for your life, you can ignore fatigue. All he could do was take another step, and another while muttering prayers that helped, over and over, keeping in rhythm with his steps.

He hoped for sleep, but that thought ended when the moon came up in a yellow globe that cast soft light through the overhang of trees. When the leader signaled the braves to move again, Elias lost hope, assuming if the neighbors had followed, they would not continue a chase during the night, and the raiders would extend their lead. He and his father and John Bigelow were on their own — with only prayer to save them.

Lord, though I walk through the valley of death. I will fear no evil. Lord though I walk...

THREE

WHEN THE SECOND evening came, and it became too dark to walk, the line finally stopped. One large, older-looking brave tied each captive against a separate tree, tightening the nooses before fastening each rawhide line. Elias's calves were burning and heels stinging with blisters, the skin on his wrists broken from the biting straps. He was still fighting back spikes of panic. There was no escaping. Ever since the initial shock of being captured, he had watched for a chance. Maybe now, in the gathering darkness, he could somehow get his hands free to untie his neck noose. But what would he do? He could not just slip away and leave his father and John. He would need a plan to free them too. He doubted he and the others would be able to outrun the devils.

Elias watched his captors huddle and finally grow still. A few lay down to sleep while others stayed close watching each prisoner. By the deepest part of the night, all but one of the natives slept, most bunched together near the edge of a tiny clearing. The three prisoners were tied close, but sleep would not come for Elias. When the guard who sat closest slumped like the others and appeared to have dozed into a shallow sleep, Elias's mind eased into dreams of home.

His mother must be frantic with worry, and he imagined her voice telling him. "Elias, you're almost a man now." She reminded him he was growing fast, and what a fine young man he was turning out to be. He had always been one of the stronger boys, feeling more like a man, and he liked when his parents and other adults treated him as one. With his voice deepening, he had begun to keep his hair long and tied in a ponytail. His skin was pale white, like all Englishmen, his face still a boy's with just a few whiskers. Now with faint hairs on his chest, he made a point of working without his shirt, so others could see.

He had always been with his father at the mill, and by the time he was fourteen, he could be counted on to perform labor necessary to cut logs into boards, his hands already calloused. His arms were thick for his age from work pulling and pushing logs into place for the saw blade. Although his father was stronger with broad shoulders, Elias had passed him in height. Working next to him, he had picked up his mannerisms, and his mother noticed.

"You remind me of your father when he was your age. I knew right away God had made him especially for me." Then she would tease, "The girls are going to fight over you some-day!" Elias liked the way his mother and others spoke to him. And how lately she hugged him for what seemed no reason.

Like other young men, Elias was born to a world with many challenges: daily survival punctuated with Indian attacks, smallpox, measles and Satan nipping at his soul. Yet for a person his age, there were bigger concerns: did he measure up — to his peers, his parents, and even someday, a wife? He could judge himself by the way he looked in a mirror — his body size, facial hair, his voice, but the real measure was the way people looked at him — how they considered him and responded when he had something to say. To be seen lacking was feared above all. Once adults considered him a man, accepted with nothing to prove, everything else — food and shelter, Indian threats, sickness, God, and even love, would take care of itself.

Now, in the deepest part of a cold night with heavy, wet dew, Elias slipped in and out of his own half-consciousness as his mind filled with thoughts of food, recalling how he had reached to slide the iron pot his mother had left snugged among the night fire's embers. When he'd dusted off the coals and lifted the lid, a sweet aroma rose while he scooped…

"Elias!" His father's whisper coaxed his mind from the dream. "Elias."

"Yes, Father."

"John Bigelow, are you with us?"

"Yes, I'm here." John's voice was thick from sleep.

"When did they get you?" Thomas asked.

"The evening before you, near the mill. They were waiting — the sly devils!"

"Did they hurt anyone?"

"No, only me. And no one saw it happen. They got away clean. We ran all night. I'm afraid to look at my blisters." After some silence, John whispered again.

"What do you think they have in mind, Thomas? I mean, what will they do to us?"

"I think they're Abenaki," answered Thomas. "The French send them to raid. If we are lucky, they will sell us back before we get too far from home." Thomas paused and then kept whispering. "Listen, we need to be careful. I don't think they would hesitate to kill us."

"How's your eye, Father? Are you all right?"

"I'm fine. They roughed me up pretty good though, but they were not counting on a fight. I think I might have broken the big one's arm."

"Yeah!" Elias whispered. "I saw it. You got 'im good!"

"They may want another chance at me before this is over. We better not give them any reasons. Stay ready and see what happens. Maybe we'll get a chance to make a break for it."

"Thomas, I'm a carpenter. You have a mill? Seems an odd coincidence, wouldn't you think?

"Hadn't thought on it, John."

"What do you think they have planned? Where are they taking us?"

"We're heading north, that's certain. That's where they will be safe. How far? I'm guess'n maybe all the way to Canada. That's probably where their big camp is. But I hope not." After several minutes, Thomas spoke again, this time in a more weary-sounding voice.

"Let's try to sleep, boys. We may be in for a long walk."

Elias tried to follow his father's advice, but his mind raced. He had heard the stories of settlers surprised in their fields, set upon by war parties, men stripped naked, with guts ripped out, their genitals carved off their bodies before they were even dead…heads crushed with hickory war clubs, family members staggering as attackers circled as if enjoying the spectacle.

Women and children were scalped and butchered in the yards — babies' smashed against tree trunks, their brains splashing onto the ground. His uncle, Ephraim, was surprised in his hayfield by over one hundred savages who shot him before slicing open his stomach.

At least they were alive. Why had they been captured? Maybe they were being led for torture! There were stories of captives tied to stakes with Indians cutting off flesh and fingers to stuff into their prisoners' mouths before burning them alive. On the Connecticut River the year before, the Deerfield settlement lost forty-eight in an attack, with over one hundred taken prisoners. Elias wondered what happened to all those people and now he understood their pain and fear.

As he shivered in the thick darkness, Lancaster felt far away, replaced by a desperate fight to live. He could only try to prepare for whatever might happen, and if the chance to escape did not come, be ready to face death…or worse.

FOUR

ELIAS WAS JERKED awake before dawn's light with the rough tug on his noose ripping him from a dream. His mouth and throat were burning, his eyes crusted and reluctant to open. In the predawn moments, just before the pink of the sun showed where it would rise, Elias tried to measure his captors. He counted eleven. The leader was the oldest — the only real adult — more mature-looking than the others. The rest of the war party included young men, not much older than himself.

When the group stopped to rest, more often now that they were far away from the whites' settlement, Elias noticed the young braves watching him as he did them, studying him, maybe with similar questions and conclusions. Their eyes would sometimes hold an awkward stare before snapping away. They murmured to each other, gesturing and laughing in a way he was sure was ridicule.

They looked similar — some with torsos covered with deer-skin — others bare. The young men were almost all shorter than himself, except for the leader. They each wore leggings with moccasin bottoms. Hatchets hung from some belts that also held long knives with bone handles tucked in scabbards. Most braves had bows, and Elias noticed his father's musket brandished by one.

With quiet steps, the group exited the thick trees and began to move along a high ridge that overlooked a valley. They were climbing along a faint trail a few paces from the high spine of a steep hill. As light increased, Elias snatched glimpses of the landscape that lay out below. He could see the outline of the horizon with the roll of hills framing the valley. Under different circumstances, he might have savored the view, but when he stumbled again, he fought the mounting despair. All his effort was to move fast enough to keep the line from snapping his neck — and to live.

Elias thought he heard the rush of water again. After a sharp turn, another river revealed itself, splashing over and around rocks, foaming and tumbling from a higher turn. The group was soon descending, their pace quickening as the terrain dropped. After they had stopped to drink, they trotted along the edge of the bank, the trail smooth and obvious. It was dark when they stopped near a mammoth boulder — a rock as high as any he had seen, near a stand of pine where they settled down to sleep. Towering pines looked much older with bigger circumferences than the trees at home. *If I get out of this, I might return to this place to hunt — land a white man has probably never seen.*

Elias had not eaten in two days and he imagined food as never before. He would eat anything. His captors had not eaten either, and Elias wondered if he might just be weak. When they ate, they must plan to feed him. Whatever the Indians had planned, it was not to starve him to death. When morning arrived, and they did not move, he thanked God; he was happy to sit. Two of the Indians scooped a shallow hole and with flint and tinder, sparked a small flame. The raiders must have finally felt safe, now in familiar territory, as if confident the settlers' pursuit had evaporated.

Later that morning, the leader signaled and sprung to an alert crouch, his gaze surveying the woods, listening for sounds no one else had heard. He moved cat-like, uncovering a musket without a sound, gliding to a different position while gesturing to direct the others. After tense moments, an Indian appeared from the woods, then another followed by over a dozen more. Near the end of the line, three children followed — two girls and an older boy, unbound but stumbling, catching up as the group filled the clearing.

With backslapping and happy greetings, the natives embraced and then began to compare their trophies. The children were white — English children — two girls in dresses with a boy in black trousers who spotted the three white men quickly. Elias thought his frightened eyes pleaded for help.

"It will be all right," Elias blurted as if to offer some comfort to the child. He waited for a reprimand from the lead Indian, but when none came, he motioned the children closer. "Come here. Who are you? What are your names?"

"I'm Simon. This is my sister, Prudence. That's our neighbor, Grace."

"What happened?" Elias asked.

"They took us — in Marlborough. We have been running ever since. A long time!"

"Us too," Elias replied, as the two girls crushed closer. The Indians' attention had slacked, so his father and John moved closer too.

"How old are you girls?" John asked.

"We're seven," replied Prudence.

"They killed my baby cousin," Grace stammered. "She was sick, so they smashed her head with a hatchet. I saw her brains all come out of her head onto the ground." Grace burst into tears and reached for John. "Are they going to kill us too? Are they?"

"They killed Mrs. Winslow too," said Simon. "And her baby. She kept crying and when we crossed a river she fell into the water; that's when an Indian hit her with his hatchet."

"It'll be alright," John promised. "Just keep up and try to stay together. Do what they tell you. We will all get home safe soon. You'll see." Elias found John's words, the first encouragement he had heard, reassuring even to himself.

Although Elias expected the group to move out, the Indians lingered. About the time the sun reached its midday zenith, two braves entered the clearing carrying a freshly killed deer hung on a pole between them. The eager group crushed close to help with the butchering. Soon the fire roared with more wood, and before long, the smell of roasting venison wafted through the campsite. When the Indians had eaten, one brave cut pieces to drop near each of the captives. Elias tore into his as if he had never eaten before, and although he could have swallowed the entire deer, it was enough — and good to eat meat.

There was no time to relax. When the food was finished, one of the Indians shouldered the deerskin, and they moved again, a group of over twenty now with three white adults and three children, picking their way through the wilderness.

FIVE

For the next many nights, the routine was the same, Mr. Sawyer estimated they had slept over twenty nights, and judging by the moon's phase, it might have been a month.

"We surely are in late November." Although it was colder, the pace of travel was more comfortable as the natives appeared more relaxed. While they walked, the braves talked with regular chatter — sometimes laughing while negotiating hills and uneven terrain. In a low place, they crossed another shallow river as they pushed north, wading through several smaller tributaries as well. Late one afternoon, they stopped at the merger of two rivers that boiled together with a great rush. Elias eased next to his father who looked as if he too was appreciating the scene. Signs of previous campfires showed this might be a regular meeting area.

Where the sun set, the pink-colored sky over the horizon turned dark purple. When the color had faded, three hunters with two more deer arrived. They were greeted with more great shouts before the group busied themselves preparing another feast.

Darkness thickened until a bright moon crept high, casting gentle, pale light over the campsite. Then all heads snapped when a surprise hail from the bushes announced another arrival. A man's excited voice boomed from behind the trees, shouting words unlike English or the grunting Elias had heard for the past many days. A bearded man emerged, loud and happy-sounding, showing neither fear nor shyness, announcing himself with confident bluster. He was white with hair long past his shoulders hanging from under a beaver skin cap. His mouth was hidden, buried under his bushy, brown beard.

Trailing behind, a small native woman followed carrying a baby strapped to her back with a wooden rack. Another child, a young girl, trotted to keep up. After hugs and greetings with the natives, the bear-like man picked out Mr. Sawyer and approached.

"Bonjour! You English? Comment ca va?"

"Yes," replied Thomas. "You're French, I see."

"Oui, Monsieur! More Indian though! Je m'appelle Maurice Pierre Montague, trader extraordinaire! Mother is Mohawk; my grandmother, she is Talise — Iroquois from near the Great Lake." The newcomer appeared to wait for the Englishmen to absorb what he had just told them. Elias could not help feeling a little better when he heard someone speaking English. Some of the Indians who had begun to gather nearby smiled as Maurice continued.

"So, my friends, let me see, can you say exactly what I may be? No? I am the mix, just like most of our people — Je suis, part of, qu'est que c'est? La grande soupe!" He laughed again, bigger this time. "This is la nouvelle France! Je suis, part of, qu'est ce que c'est? La grande soupe!" He laughed again, bigger. "La grande casserole!"

Maurice was a big talker. Hearing him jumble his excited words with French, English and Indian, Elias liked the man right away.

"Englishmen!" he bellowed. "You were not careful, no? Got yourself caught in how you say, the snare? What is your home?"

"Lancaster, in the Massachusetts Bay Colony."

"Each of you?"

"Yes, this is my son, Elias," said Thomas. "And here is John Bigelow."

"Can you get us food?" asked John. "We're starving."

"Oui," said Maurice. "But you are still alive, no? They will not let you die now."

"It's been days," said Thomas, and we are very weak. Can you talk to them? You seem like friends."

"Yeah," said John. "We need something…anything!"

Maurice nodded to agree and asked again about where they lived. "You are Bostoniak then? Near the eastern sea?"

"No, not close," said Thomas. "Thirty miles inland — in the woods. Do you know the Nashaway?"

"No, I am not familiar with that land." Maurice stretched his arms and continued. "I am born and lived twenty-seven snows, only in these woods — at the Sault Saint Louis, the rapids on la Rivière Saint Louis. My aunt and her family live there still — near the mission.

"Is that close?" asked John.

"Many more days," said Maurice.

Elias was curious. "You speak many languages, Maurice? How do you know English so well?"

"Ah, mon ami, une neccessite! I trade often with your English in Al-ban-ee. They pay much for furs. We make good trade."

"What do these raiders want with us?" asked Thomas.

"Yes, and what about the children?" asked John. "Why did they take them?"

"These children, they adopt. It has been the Indian way for generations. A few, like you, might be ransomed. The little ones always fetch the best price." Maurice seemed to savor the stage as he continued explaining the Indians' culture. "Plenty of women will want these little girls to raise, and the boy, he will fit nicely into a family as well. He is just the right size so as not to give them the trouble — just do his work. They can always use more braves." Maurice paused and surveyed the group of Indians before continuing. "Because many of their young do not survive, families need more children — to satisfy their women. They cry for their dying babies. Some captives might be returned to English families, but many decide to stay. You know of this?"

Decide to stay? Elias looked for the three children who had joined their group the previous morning. They were not bound like the men and were busy eating with Maurice's wife, huddled close to the only woman in the camp. They were dirty, the girls' hair was snarled but otherwise they did not seem as frightened as before. Elias thought, for children, a full belly and a mother must be medicine in any language.

"Don't worry gentlemen, I don't think your enemy plans to hurt you — but only if you behave. They just want the money you are worth to the French. Or to your families. Your ransom will buy many muskets. I do hope your kin love you!" With a chuckle at his joke, he turned and rejoined the Indians. He left Elias, Thomas and John grinning as if they had enjoyed a gift, because Le Grand Trapper, with all his talking and lecturing and his easy, confident spirit, had just given the frightened, starving captives hope.

Elias was tied to a tree, sitting with a rawhide rope pinching his neck. When food smells drifted from the fire, he struggled to control himself, straining his tether like a dog as his captors gorged on turkey and moose meat he had watched them turn so long over the fire. He had never known hunger, not real hunger, not like this — hunger that had replaced every other thought, as if he might never be satisfied again.

The Indians, with Maurice and his family moving among them, shared meat as it became ready. Maurice's wife carved strips for her husband and the children while each brave helped himself. When the men were satisfied, two braves carried meat strips to John, Elias and his father. The biggest Indian followed, standing as if amused to watch his famished prisoners tear at their meat. Maurice was interested as well, moving close to stand beside the big Indian. Elias had been noticing how the leader controlled the group with his stern demeanor and intense looks. He looked always angry and on guard as if anticipating a challenge or attack.

"This is a big man," announced Maurice. "Matunaagd — it means 'great fighter.' His grandfather's name was the same. His braves just call him Matun." Maurice seemed eager to show the prisoners his understanding of things. "His grandfather was a great chief who fought the English many times in the south. He

25

may be chief someday. He's already one of their best raiders, I'm told." Elias thought Maurice was trying to flatter the Indian as he added even more in Indian tongue.

"Matun, this is John. And this man, he is Thomas Sawyer. His son, Elias is here." The Indian did not acknowledge the captives but spoke directly to Maurice using French words combined with Indian phrases. Elias tried to decipher the attitudes, strange speech and tenor of the dialogue, but Matun's words were a mystery.

Maurice listened to the Indian and then moved closer to the captives to translate.

"Well, men, I can see you are wondering, so here is exactly what Matun says."

'I tell you, Maurice, these English we sell. Francais, they pay us well — many musket. This Thomas, he makes the big fight. We keep him for no trade. Our chief, he will say it so.'"

While Elias wondered what it all could mean, he was startled when John addressed Maurice with a challenge for the Indian.

"Ask him why they attack us and kill our people?" Maurice considered the request with a glance toward Matun but responded in a soothing tone without passing the question.

"You see, my English friend, it is a business,"

"Some business!" John barked without stopping gnawing at his bone. "Go ahead, Maurice, ask him why they attack our people."

The trapper appeared skilled at diffusing, straddling middle ground, ignoring John while his foolish attack faded. It was obvious Maurice had practiced living safely between two worlds without taking sides while considering the limits of the

Indians' patience.

Matun had walked several strides, but with John's angry tone, he stopped, turning his head and shoulders, his face showing exaggerated surprise. With his gaze fixed on Maurice, he finished his turn and began a slow return to the prisoners. He passed Maurice, continuing to John who had struggled to his feet. Matun removed an eight-inch blade from its scabbard and with his face almost touching John's, pressed the point against his prisoner's neck.

Maurice inched closer to Matun, addressing him with indistinguishable words in a soft, measured voice. The warrior responded by lowering the knife and stepping back — examining John — measuring him. Then Matun surprised everyone when he leaned close and cut the rawhide binding from John's hands. With a look at Maurice, then to his men, Matun did the same for Elias and Thomas. Then he offered John his knife, handle first, lifting John's hand, insisting he grasp the weapon until John complied. Then as if bored with the encounter, Matun turned and approached his men who had by now left the fire and come close to see the show. When they met, Matun turned and with arms extended, challenged John with a booming voice.

"Allez, Allez! Go, English! Allez! The braves all pushed past Matun toward John, laughing and taunting, encouraging John to run. "Allez, Allez!"

Despite the excited voices, Thomas spoke to John, his words steady and calm.

"Drop the knife, John." John did not move. "John, just drop it — then sit down."

As Elias held his breath, the knife finally dropped, and John turned and squatted. With a slight head-gesture from Matun, a brave scampered to retrieve the knife while two more trotted to John. While continuing a barrage of taunting words, one brave pushed John over before both began punching and slapping their prisoner who curled on the ground with his arms covering his head. When Matun barked again, they stopped and returned to the fire.

Thomas and the Elias eased close to comfort their friend.

Thomas was first to speak. "Are you hurt, John?"

"I'll be alright," John grumbled.

"You won't be alright, John. None of us will be alright if you cannot keep your mouth shut."

"They'll pay for that, Thomas. The first chance I get."

Only when Matun and all the braves had moved out of earshot did Maurice come to the prisoners, crouching close, whispering to his new friends.

"Be careful, English. You have been lucky. But I tell you, these people have no patience with captives. I have seen." Maurice's cheerful persona was gone. "Please, mes amies, do not make Matun angry, or, how you say, underestimate him — his capacity or resolve. Leave your pride behind. Do what you must to survive." Maurice paused his gaze at each, locking eyes as if making sure his words were having the desired impact. He continued slowly. "I cannot save any of you." The trapper waited before completing his advice. "Do not challenge! And above all, do not try to escape!" He removed his hat, glanced at the fire and scratched under the thick hair over his ear as if preparing his last words. "If you do, and you are caught, which I tell you is certain, they will torture you. Comprenez-vous?" No one spoke. "And when that is finally done, I have seen this, they will watch you burn."

With the warning complete, John, Elias and his father remained silent, as if lost in their fear. The trapper ambled back to the big fire, joining his native friends whose banter and laughter continued. Later, when the captors' group quieted settling down for the night, Elias rubbed his wrists, enjoying the feeling of free hands again. With the small liberty and his hunger diminished, he could not help feeling strangely relieved — as if he could let himself hope the worst might be over. He let himself go, as if slipping out of his nightmare into the first real sleep since his capture.

SIX

WHILE THEY WALKED and camped many more nights, the party swelled with additional raiders and captives they encountered along the way. Elias counted more than thirty, including Maurice and his family. He measured himself against his captors, wondering what they might be thinking. Simon fell in close behind him as they traveled, and they talked while they walked. Elias tried to ease the boy's fears, assuring him that if they did as they were told and did not make a fuss, they would surely all see their families again.

"How old are you, Simon?"

"Almost nine." The boy moved closer to Elias.

"I'm sixteen," Elias said. "What is your surname?"

"Fairbanks."

Elias was reluctant to ask about the boy's parents, but he didn't need to.

"Father and mother are dead." Simon's voice rose high-pitched to the beginning of a cry. "I think so. When we were leaving, I looked back and saw them on the ground lying still. I wish I were dead too."

"You need to live, Simon. Be strong. Your sister needs you now. You will have to be a man sooner than you thought." When Elias said it, it was as if he were talking to himself. Since the capture, Elias felt he had left what remained of boyhood behind.

With the sun moving past noon, the countryside was ablaze with crimson and yellow of fall foliage mixed on a canvas of green. Elias sensed the fullness of the forest, the rolling hills and views sparkling with brilliant color. On some vistas, clumps of brilliant white birch trees sparkled, contrasting the forest's dark shade. Since many of the trees near home had been cut for building or firewood, Elias began noticing the size of the pines, many with a circumference larger than two men's arms could surround. They were majestic, towering high overhead, forming a tangled canopy that shut out direct sunlight. Smaller, plump evergreens snuggled beneath, each with a full dress of green branches, their tops dotted with brown pinecones.

Days began to feel shorter as their group continued north, dipping into low valleys that left the sun behind high horizons until late morning and again blocking rays as it disappeared behind the trees each evening. It was colder too; the ground had gotten harder. Then it started to rain. As if by a marker, fall season ended, and winter approached with cold rain falling either in occasional gentle drizzle or a punishing downpour. Each day they kept moving.

When four hunters arrived carrying a moose they had slung over a pole, everyone shouted with joy, while some scurried to prepare a fire. After they had eaten, Maurice came over where they huddled, this time with introductions. From under his cloak, the proud-looking trapper presented an infant boy.

"Le voici! My son, not ten months! And he almost walks!" Maurice squatted before shifting and helping the boy stand within the circle of his arms. "I am going to teach him well — to be the grandest trapper of us all!"

"He's a handsome lad, Maurice," said Mr. Sawyer. "I will admit that." For Elias, it was good to see his father's interest and see him grinning again. "If you lived with us, Maurice, I might make a good millwright out of him."

"Mais non!" laughed Maurice. "This boy will never know anything but life in these woods — the rivers, the hills, the beaver — and our friends, the Indians. This world is all a man needs."

"There is more to life than the woods," said John.

"That's what English think; we French-Indian know better. Meet my wife, Angeni Bouat. She is part Missoula, part Abenaki — even some French. Her grandfather was French Voyageur, just like me." Maurice's wife was covered with a deerskin shawl that hung from her shoulders to below her knees. Fringe on the bottom accented deerskin leggings that merged into moccasins. Her black hair was confined in two rope-like braids. She had shed the wooden baby cradle. Her lips formed a warm-looking, gentle smile at each of the men. A tiny girl wiggled from behind, slipping past her mother's leg to clutch at her father's arm, hugging the big man before turning her head and attention to the adults from her safe place. Maurice's face exploded in a big grin before he hugged and kissed the squirming little girl.

"This is Fidilia, my Petite Flying Bird! She is four." The tiny girl was covered in deerskin with the blackest, straight hair falling down her back. "Can you see, Messieurs, before you this happy man? And so are many more like me. We have the lives men should!" While he spoke, he twisted and sometimes tossed his young son in the air, catching him the same way Elias saw fathers in Lancaster do with a tickling hug, burying his face in the child's neck to make him laugh and squeal.

"Come on, my little turtle, let's all go to the fire. It's time we all got some sleep. I will see you men with the next sun; we have a lot more walking to do tomorrow." As he moved away, Maurice turned his head and threw more advice over his shoulder. "Get some rest, my English friends; you will need it!"

SEVEN

THE NEW ENVIRONMENT was so different than home: Elias was cold. His breath often smoked out in a winter cloud from his mouth, and it seemed the months had raced ahead. When the rain stopped, it turned even colder. They were always wet, as they crossed brooks and large streams often. Sometimes they would wade through a river, the braves plunging ahead over their shoulders. Not until night could they dry their clothes by the fire and begin to be warm again. After they had traveled six more days, flurries of snow covered everything with a thin, white veil. Although he was weak, Elias preferred walking — at least that kept him warm. Shallow sleep did not renew his vigor but only reminded him of food and his gnawing hunger. *What about these raiders? They must be hungry and tired too.* And they showed no signs of fatigue, only enthusiasm and determination.

The captured children remained frightened and unsure, often crying. Simon had adopted Elias as if his guardian, and the girls, Prudence and Grace, never left the side of Maurice's wife.

"Looks like our new family has grown," said John as he worked at drying his pants by the fire. "Makes me homesick for my own."

Elias and his father looked at each other with surprised faces.

"You have children, John?"

"I do — four. My boy and girl are the same age as Maurice's. I have Jerusha — she's eight, Thankful, she's six, Joseph is two and my baby, John, he just turned one."

"Why didn't you say something?"

"I don't know, Thomas. Maybe it was just my way of protecting them. I can't imagine these animals getting near them." Before Thomas or Elias could ask more questions, John's shoulders hunched, and he turned away as if to choke off emotion. After some silence, he continued as if trying to explain. "This is killing me. My wife is twenty-eight; I'm just thirty. We have our life ahead. I cannot die here. I have to escape."

"We'll all get back soon, John. Remember what Maurice told us. Let's just work together and stay strong." When John remained quiet, Thomas pushed. "We won't consider anything foolish, right John?"

"Don't worry Thomas. I plan to live to see my wife and children again." Then John changed the subject. "I reckon we must have traveled two hundred miles by now. We must be getting close to Canada, wouldn't you think?"

"Probably right." Thomas's voice was sure, belying any hint of discomfort or concern for their situation. Although fifty-six, his body was more like a young man's with a big upper body, thick biceps and strong hands calloused from a lifetime of labor. He was the first of thirteen children who at an early age had developed confidence, determination and a leader's instincts.

After Maurice's warning, Elias realized escape was out of the question. Even if they could slip away, they would starve. But more likely, they would be re-captured, and he did believe Maurice — they would be killed. He somehow endured each day, with conversations not unlike others they might have at home or the mill — about their new companions, their families, what they would each do when they returned. And what they planned to eat.

"I'm going to butcher my fattest hog," said Thomas, "invite my entire family for the biggest feast Lancaster has ever seen!"

"You better kill two, Thomas! One for your family — the other one just for me!"

"I might go through all the squash myself," laughed Elias.

As they traveled, they were joined by several more raiding parties, most with prisoners. The forest was teeming with native people. They stopped at promontories overlooking valleys and twisting rivers of all sizes, all flowing north. They would sometimes skirt a river backwater or pond. There were lodges and marks of beaver everywhere with trees gnawed through, dropped into the water and across streams. Green mountain laurel patches accented the brush. The woods were dark as if spirits might live there. With sunlight blocked by the dense tree canopy, the forest floor was spongy — green and damp — growing with heavy moss like a carpet spread over the ground, every inch covered with something alive. For Elias, the gloomy woods felt foreboding, like a mysterious tunnel, gray light falling like a curtain that prevented clear sight ahead.

Lancaster was different — brighter in the woods with sunlight and trails and open spaces. Early settlers had learned Indians had for centuries burned the underbrush, leaving the landscape a delight, like a park in England, easy to navigate with trails the English adopted and expanded to cart paths. However, these northern woods felt virgin, cluttered with fallen, rotting trees crisscrossed throughout, making moving in a straight line difficult. The Indians were at home, picking their way along faint but familiar paths that twisted through the woods. The leader had surely made this journey before following an almost invisible, generations-old trail.

The woods were dotted with enormous gray boulders as well, towering over their heads. They passed remains of campsites, usually where one brook fed into another. Quiet was severe, but after they had camped and began to settle, the birds became less timid with calls, and the occasional screech of blue jays sparked from the trees. Squirrels scampered through the branches high overhead, throwing down chatter. With darkness, the night's quiet was broken with calls of hoot owls and occasional howls of wolves or coyotes.

They were seldom alone, passing men and women emerging unexpectedly from an unseen trail or sliding by on a river in dirty-looking, dug-outs or bright, white birch bark canoes. The prisoners' journey began to feel more leisurely with increased contact with others. All wore deerskin leggings, while women, like Maurice's wife, were appearing more often, covered with deer-skin frocks down to their shins, the same as Maurice's wife. The parties always stopped for conversation, including much pointing and gesturing at the captives. The new arrivals took great interest in each, easing closer for better looks. Elias returned the stares and even encouraged them closer. Despite their situation, Elias thought the young men could not be that much different than himself. But when he tried to communicate with the braves, they returned only icy stares.

"You, what's your name?" he asked. With no response, he spoke to another brave, but the Indian looked at the others, as if for permission to respond. There were only a few grunts and nasty looks.

"Come over, I won't bite. Come here. What, are you afraid of me?" The more confident moved close and sometimes reached to feel the cloth of his shirt. One evening, the fire had been larger, surrounded by about fifty Indians enjoying another feast of moose. It had been raining for a few days, and Elias, John, and his father, with Maurice, his wife and children, crushed especially close to the flames to dry their clothes, while their captors, not as wary, allowed them closer to share the heat.

Elias slipped off his boots and pushed them close enough to dry but not too close to burn. The skin on his heels was raw and hurt, but at least they were not getting any worse. The same toe on each foot had a broken blister. His pants hung loose on his hips, and he could sense his weight loss, his shoulders feeling especially bony when he lay on his side at night.

One of the young braves sauntered close to the fire, and with exaggerated bluster, examined Elias' boot, turning it end for end, running his hand over the heel. Elias watched, and when their eyes met, Elias gestured to offer the second boot. The brave sat near his friends and slipped on the boots. When he stood, he stumbled while he tried to walk closer to Elias.

"Magus," said the brave, pointing to himself.

"Me, Elias Sawyer. He is John Bigelow. This is my father, Thomas Sawyer." His new acquaintance continued with introductions, pointing at each brave as if to pull them into the conversation. "C'est Claude-Thomas. C'est Saksarie. C'est Nikora. Rowi. Roussin."

Elias's father and John watched, sharing glances. They were tired, cold, starved, and afraid, but it was as if the young men had given them a gift. A small, silly thing, but Elias was certain it was good for everyone — to feel human again. It was enough, for the moment at least, just to feel alive.

EIGHT

BEFORE SLIVERS OF light made the dawn sky pink above the trees, they started again. Their captors' excitement increased probably as their home grew closer. Later that day when they'd crested a small hill, the forest opened, and they looked down at water stretching far to the horizon.

"Is that the ocean?" Elias asked.

"No!" laughed Maurice. "That's the St. Lawrence River. Follow it that way." He pointed east. "The ocean is waiting. That is what the People say."

They stood near a precipice, a cliff high above the land below. The terrain was cleared for a great distance, sloping away from the river's shore. A village stretched from the water's edge back toward the forest with scores of small black specks — round huts bunched together with thin, black smoke rising from each.

"This is it, gentlemen!" Maurice took the stage with an exaggerated sweep of his arm. "Say hello to New France!"

Near the horizon, on a promontory, a sharp-looking building towered over the surrounding landscape. Large gray stones
formed walls. Spiking from the middle, a tall tower lifted high
above the treetops.

"What's the big building?" John asked. "With all the
stones?"

"That's the Sillery — the Jesuit mission."

"The builders knew what they were doing," said John as
they began to follow the trail that slipped down the long slope
to the river. "Quite impressive."

"Yes, the French came early. They built a fort downriver in
case the English got ideas — or the Dutch. They were exploring
here as well long ago."

"There must be a hundred huts down there," said Elias.

"They're wigwams. There are hundreds up and down the
river. The big ones are longhouses — they hold a few families."

"Who lives here?"

"Who? Oh, my! All kinds. Abenaki from the east. And
people the Dutch called Mohicans — the Mohawk — the 'Bear
Place People.'

"Now what happens, Maurice?" asked John. "To us. What
will they do with us?"

"We still have a way to go. Maybe Montreal tomorrow. Or
next. Then you meet Indian hosts. Probably Pukeewis, the
chief. He will need a good look at you. Then he will parley to
make a good trade. The French governor, he will settle the
price."

It was becoming more obvious to Elias that Maurice was a
friend they could trust and was genuinely interested in helping
his new friends.

"Mes amies, we will just have to wait and see how many muskets the French think you're worth — and jugs of the brandy."

NINE

THE DOME-LIKE WIGWAMS were made of saplings bent together in frames, covered by birch bark, deerskin and moss. Some wigwams were long, about the size of four or five combined. As the prisoners approached a small hut, the lead brave threw back the entrance flap before Elias, Thomas and John bent to enter, pushed through by a guard.

It was dark inside, like a cave, but the dirt floor was dry with a cushion of leaves. In the center, a pit held stones for a fire. With the low ceiling, a man would need to sit but could stand in the middle under a hole in the roof left for the smoke to exit. Although they could move about, they waited for their eyes to adjust to the dark. When two young Indians brought food and a burning branch to start the fire, the wigwam warmed quickly, and Elias began to feel better about things. The next morning, he was happy to see Maurice arrive at the wigwam, although the trapper was not his usual, happy-looking self.

"Mes amies," Maurice began with a strangely somber voice, "I'm afraid I have some troubling news." Maurice was accompanied by four strong-looking braves who stood close while watching the trapper carefully. "Matun is angry — at John."

"At me? What did I do?"

Maurice did not respond to John directly as he continued in a stern, determined-sounding voice.

"I've discovered he wants to punish you, Thomas, instead — for John's behavior — and for hurting one of his braves at your mill." John and Thomas stared at each other until Maurice continued. "It seems Chief Pukeewis may allow Matun to have his way." Maurice hesitated when they crushed closer to hear the rest. "I'm sorry to have to say this, my friends, but, you see, they have this custom." Maurice stammered and stopped, with his gaze focused on his feet before he forced his words out almost in a whisper. "Matun wants to watch you die."

"Die!" John blurted.

"Kill him?" shrieked Elias. "For what?"

"Why?" asked Thomas.

"He says you are 'big warrior — much strong.' You broke Mantak's arm, and his brother Rogierre has much pain in his neck from your fight."

"Hey!" shouted Thomas. "What did they expect? They got what they asked for!"

"It's not that easy. They have their ways — mysterious maybe but big trouble for you. There's not too much we can do about it."

"Let's make a run for it," said John. "Get to the French. There must be someone we can talk to."

"I've tried seeing Chief Pukeewis, but his braves won't have it. I can only push so far, Thomas." Elias moved to embrace his father, fighting back tears.

"Father!" he cried. "What can we do? Come on, we've got to do something!" His father accepted Elias's embrace but spun out of his grasp to address the trapper.

"Who's in charge here, Maurice?"

"The French — they control — from Quebec City. For the People, theirs is only a loose alliance — a shaky one. The French, they suggest only. And they are careful not to, qu'est-ce que c'est, "the feathers to ruffle!" The men did not seem patient with the trapper's word jumble.

"I tried, Thomas, believe me. I tried. But I am a no-one. It seems what Matun wants, he usually gets." As he reached for the flap to leave the wigwam, Maurice paused and tossed the men something to hold onto.

"I'm going to try to get to the Jesuits. It might be a chance. My aunt lives near the mission; she has a friend whose cousin is a nun there. I can only say it's worth a try. Maybe someone can help. If not, we must hope this is like the wind, and over us she blows. Maybe the chief reconsiders."

"Could he," pleaded Elias, "reconsider?"

"Maybe. There is, after all, what should be a hearty ransom. I wasn't expecting them to give that up so easily." As Maurice was leaving, dropping his head to duck through the opening, he remarked with a sideways glance, "Gentlemen, if I were you, I would ask your English God for help. If he did follow you here, maybe he is listening!"

TEN

T HE THREE CAPTIVES knelt in the middle of the wigwam as Thomas led them in prayer.

"Heavenly Father," he began in slow, halting words, "your will has carried us to this captivity... and you've kept us safe to this point. Since it is your plan, we accept it. But in your goodness and mercy, we beg you to spare our family the grief my death would create. Surely you can prevail on the minds of the savages as they too ..." Thomas stammered and then stopped. When Elias started to cry, John took over.

"God, smite the devil that has captured the souls of these savages! Show them your power and wrath!"

"Please, Lord," Elias begged. "If you would just grant this wish, to spare my father's life, I'll do anything! I promise! I'll follow your teachings always, for the rest of my life!" Through his loud sobs, Elias struggled to finish his prayer. "Please, God Almighty! Please!"

After a long silence, Thomas resumed in a more composed

tone.

"Lord, let these souls find your blessings and mercy, accept your teachings and abandon their terrible inclination for murder and mayhem. In God's name, we pray. Amen."

After they had joined in "Amen," the wigwam was silent, each man lost in his thoughts. Elias searched his soul for the strength to meet this test with more instinct to escape. *How can I allow my father to be killed? I'll be ready to fight when they come!*

"We have to run, John!"

"No use, Elias." John was busy near the exit and mumbled as he peeked out the flap. I count at least five out there. And they've all got hatchets."

Their conversation waned as the hours dragged through the long night. They had not slept when at dawn several braves surprised them, storming into the wigwam with hatchets held high, separating the men with shouts and threats. When they pulled Thomas outside, two men looped a noose around the neck of John and then Elias, then pulled them along behind. A group of cheering women circled the men, moving alongside as Thomas was hurried along. Their taunting and howling were severe while they tried to strike Elias and John with long sticks as they passed. The guards forced Thomas forward to a gathering point in the middle of the village before stopping at a stake extending from a pile of wood. *This cannot be happening!* As Elias strained the rawhide ties around his wrists, he begged with a loud cry.

"God help us! Please God, I am begging you! Save my father!"

While the crowd swelled, Thomas was pinned against the

post and held by four braves. His feet were strapped, his arms pulled behind the stake and re-tied. The cries of the gathered natives rose and charged the air with excitement. A desperate Elias screamed for his father, and then John and even for Maurice.

"Maurice! Maurice! Help, Maurice! Stop them!" But Maurice stood apart, swallowed into the crowd with his wife and children, powerless to intercede. While Pukeewis addressed the group, Elias and John tried to understand the words and follow what was happening. Maurice left his family to ease close to Elias and John.

"Be strong, Elias. Remember, your father as a brave man."

"No! You cannot! Stop! Let him go!" Elias had begun to sob again and did not try to hide it. "You Savages! You cowards! Please God, help us! Please, I beg you!" Elias had lost all control. *My God, what have I done? Why have you abandoned me?*

As the excited crowd crushed closer to the woodpile, more women joined the men with children squirming forward through the crowd to watch the show.

"You son-of-a-bitches!" John's voice rose above the others. "You filthy savages! You cowards! Why don't you fight like men?" His cries produced no effect. "Where is your humanity? Where is your decency? You devils! You'll pay for this!"

The braves must have heard enough. They forced John and Elias to the ground using their clubs for blows to their prisoners' heads and shoulders and the backs of their knees. Elias's entire body racked as he buried his face into his sleeve and sobbed.

"Father!" he cried. "God! Please, God. Please!"

While Elias lay curled and sobbing on the ground, a brave emerged from the crowd and with the peoples' rising cheers, leaned to touch a flaming torch to the pile of wood.

ELEVEN

"HEATHEN!" THE VOICE thundered across the heads of the people in the crowd. The festivities stopped with a sound like a thunderclap or a cannon explosion. Everyone froze while they looked at each other in wonderment as if awakened by sounds in the night. The excitement and noise were replaced with a strange stillness as each person swiveled their gaze as if trying to locate the voice that demanded attention.

"Heathen! I command you! Release this man!" Elias staggered to his feet, and as he wiped his eyes on his sleeves, his crying stopped.

"Look, Elias!" shouted Maurice. "It's a priest! A Jesuit!"

Hope flickered in Elias, as he could see the man in black had the attention of the people.

"Heathen, hear me! I hold the key to Purgatory! With it, I will open the gates, and you will all be swallowed into the fires of damnation unless you release this man!" He was French and a priest, it was clear. His black beard was long, and his hair flowed over his shirt collar. With his black robe swirling and hiding his feet, he held a shining key aloft while he moved into the crowd. The religious man must have had plenty of practice holding attention while his loud words were the only sounds.

"The Great Father in heaven has entrusted me with this key and instructed me to use it today to open the gates to damnation. Release this man, or the devil will come to escort you into hell!" Silence and fear hung in the air as the natives shrunk back, and then, with more commands from the priest, they began to retreat even further. Maurice jumped and clapped, cheering in support of the savior.

"Listen to the words of the Holy Man!" he cried. "Listen to him!"

"Untie him!" boomed the priest. "By all the souls in heaven, I command you to untie this man!" No one moved. "Great Chief, Pukeewis! I command you! Do as the greatest God has instructed. Cut this man loose! Free him now!"

Pukeewis hesitated, but when he made the slightest of gestures, two braves scurried to untie Thomas and help him struggle down from the top of the wood pile.

"Come, my Son," coaxed the priest. "Come to me, and I will protect you. Our God has spoken through me."

"That's a Jesuit," Maurice explained as he crushed closer to Elias and John. You can thank your God he got here in time." The Jesuit continued his performance, holding the key high like a weapon. Then he shouted as if to end his speech.

"The Great God has spoken." They were his last words as people parted like water, allowing him to lead Elias's father deeper into the settlement and out of sight.

Elias felt empty, drained from the emotional ordeal. But by now he was used to physical fatigue. As the crowd dispersed, and he and John began the walk back to the wigwam, he avoided others' eyes — even his guards'. He felt stained with shame. *How could I have acted like a child?* He had given up, curled on the ground while tears ran down his cheeks.

"Come on, Elias. You should be happy! Don't you see? God is with us; he's answered our prayers!" But despite John's enthusiasm, Elias knew he had failed. Through the ordeal of the attack and the journey from Lancaster — the fear, the hunger, the cold — he was considering himself more of a man, especially in his father's and other's eyes. But his self-confidence had been erased in a few moments of weakness and defeat. It would take a long time to regain the status he felt he had earned. At least his family and the people at home would never know, and he was determined to bury this failure. Whatever happened from now on, he would never act like anything but a man.

TWELVE

E LIAS AND JOHN were returned to the same wigwam where they remained under guard until the next morning when a boy, about ten, appeared. He wore deerskin leggings and moccasins, and his torso was covered by a thick, English, linen jacket, much like what Elias and other boys wore at home. Accompanied by the guards, Elias and John followed the youth in the direction the priest and his father had taken the day before. As they walked, the settlement crushed around them with a thicker, more permanent-looking arrangement of structures punctuated with signs and shops. Worn paths spoked from a small square where white men and women moved among Indians. As they passed, Elias heard bits of French and Indian conversations along with the metal ringing from a blacksmith shop's hammer. They entered a larger market area with people milling and talking, barely taking notice of what must have been a curious-looking group moving along.

The houses of the compound were mostly wood, but several were built with stone. After what could have been a mile, they climbed an incline approaching a three-story, stone building at the highest point of land. They followed stone steps to a heavy-looking wooden entrance. When they had opened the door and slipped into a large hallway, the smell and gentle, warm touch of a fireplace met them, reminding Elias of home. A small Indian woman greeted them and suggested they sit in several stuffed chairs in a waiting room off the hallway. They had not settled long before Elias's father appeared accompanied by three bearded white men.

"Gentlemen, welcome to New France! I am Father Louis Pierre Thury, Bishop of Quebec. Let me introduce Father Gilbert, Monseigneur of Saint-Vallier Mission. And this is Father Francois Mittot from our newest mission — above the rapids — The Sault Saint-Louis. We are Jesuits."

"Welcome, English. I am Father Francois — your interpreter. I will try to recall the English words I learned as a student in London."

Elias spoke up.

"Father Louis, thank you for saving my father." While the men shook hands, John and Thomas added "thank-yous."

"You are safe for now," the priest responded, "but you're still the property of Matun with the approval of his chief. You are his prisoners to do with what he wishes. But at least you will not be killed."

"What will happen to us?" John asked.

"Governor Vaudreuil will meet with you soon. He will broker a settlement with Chief Pukeewis. But today is for us to give God thanks and get acquainted; we will break bread and pray together. It's not often we can enjoy the company of other white brethren, even if you are Englishmen."

Religious displays were everywhere with paintings of robed men on the walls, wearing large crucifixes like the little ones at the end of the black beads hanging from the Fathers' waists. The men surrounded a large dining table where native attendants served plates of steaming food: meat, fish, corn and squash, pheasant, bread, and wine. As the captives ate their first real meal in many weeks, Father Gilbert addressed his guests.

"Our missionaries came to this Saint Lawrence long before any of us were born. The first Jesuits sailed the river in 1642."

"The French have been here much longer than that," Father Francois added. "The king sent Jacques Cartier to find a Northwest Passage to Asia."

"Please, gentlemen," said Father Louis. "Eat! We have plenty more. Here, try this young bird."

"Québec City is very old, before your *Mayflower*!" Father Gilbert laughed, clearly relishing the stage and the attention of the visitors. "With God's grace, we will continue to expand and survive for many more generations to come. I am proud to say, earlier this year Father Rale established our newest mission, St. Xavier at Becancour. We have big plans."

The priests acted as if enjoying the company and the chance to talk about many things, even if much of the conversation was being passed through the interpreter. John and Thomas did not say much. Elias suspected, like him, they were half-listening, more interested in eating than conversation.

"Here!" offered Father Gilbert. "You must try this. It is the syrup de maple; the natives make it each spring. Pour it on your squash. They have provided everything — from their fields and the forest."

"The corn is my favorite," Father Louis said.

As the men filled their stomachs, the plates began to pass less, but the waiters continued delivering more food while Father Gilbert continued.

"We have an alliance with the Wabanaki — every tribe. Four years ago we signed a treaty, 'Le Grand Peace de Montreal.'" When Father Gilbert stopped talking, stabbed more pieces of venison, and Father Louis took over.

"Two hundred canoes came down the river, all the way from the great lakes of the west — thirteen hundred braves — representatives from forty native nations. All came to Montreal to arrange a truce between all the tribes."

"Possibly the biggest peace conference in history!" Father Francois added. As Elias listened, his father and John appeared more interested now that their stomachs were finally full.

"Amazing," John said as he reached for another corn. "Some parley, no?"

The men laughed.

"Yes, in New France we live together with our native brethren. Algonquin mostly, come here to get away from the Iroquois — fleeing east. Many came from your area as well — Pequot tribe survivors and remnants of the Wampanoags — those your soldiers did not kill. The French government and we Jesuits take good care of them; they are safe here."

"How?" asked John. "How are they safe?"

"We make sure they have food, and other tribes do not bother them. The Indians know we want to convert them, and we know, for the most part, many just play along. But they fight for the French too. We have much in common — we need each other. And we protect each other from your English soldiers."

"Why?" asked Elias. "Why are we fighting?"

"Why?" The priest's face assumed a thoughtful expression. "Maybe you'll get a chance to find out. The Indians can tell you all about the massacres. Believe me, my young friend, they have plenty of stories."

John interrupted.

"I could tell you a few stories, Father. They've butchered plenty of our people."

"I don't doubt you, mon ami, but have you ever stopped to think why?" The men waited.

"You see, the French and English have been killing each other for centuries. But now the war is not only in Europe with Dutch and English fighting France and Spain. Generals marching to grand battles with great bluster, flags and cannons booming, the same way armies have battled for generations. Now it is 'Queen Anne's War,' and it has come to this continent."

"Voici comment c'est," added Father Gilbert, "le natural order?"

Father Francois continued. "The real contest is here, in the new world. These people are remnants of those that were here before. European disease has decimated the population — over half — measles and smallpox, that is what the white man has brought. And so, the balance has been disturbed. But Quebec is safe because the French protect them. That is why they help to fight the English. You are their real enemy."

"We wouldn't be if they didn't attack us," said John.

"Oh, come now. Mr. Bigelow." The Father spoke in a more condescending tone. "Surely, Sir, you are not that naïve. And you, Mr. Sawyer, you have a mill, do you not — to cut boards to build houses for your neighbors?"

"That's right."

"And those neighbors plant corn and raise animals to feed their families, oui?"

"Of course."

"What do you tell the people who used to hunt where your new house may be, or where your corn grows? Do you tell them to come to hunt with friends whenever they please?"

"They sold us the land," barked John.

"Of course, they did!" laughed the Father. "Of course. You see, gentlemen that is the problem, no — in le 'nutshell'? The English have come to this new world for one reason — land. And the people that are here? They are in the way. Unfortunately," he finished with a mock laugh, "English do not share well."

"Here." Father Francois changed the mood. "Have more squash. It's my favorite." Elias was growing a bit tired of the talk, although he had to agree, the squash was excellent. But John did not let the subject drop.

"What you mean, Father, is that you manipulate the savages to do your bidding." The Father paused before replying to John's surprise advance with a more measured, confident-sounding voice.

"Believe me, Mr. Bigelow, the Indian chiefs have learned what has happened in New England — how the Penobscot and others were annihilated by your militia. A few survivors live with us. Stories of massacres and atrocities are told and retold in lodges here and as far away as the big lakes of the west. Entire villages were put to the torch, everyone killed, hundreds at a time — even women and children. And those who were not killed were sold into slavery."

"That was long ago," said Thomas.

"Only a generation, Mr. Sawyer. Believe me, the native people have learned what hides in the hearts of the English. But we French, we do not want to hurt these people. We show them the way to heaven; we only want their souls."

"Their souls?" scoffed John. He sounded angry. "Is that what you call it? Your religion is designed for creating servants — even mercenaries."

"Our religious differences prevent us from the same interpretations, Mr. Bigelow. Englais and Francais, we see the world differently and fear each other's God. Do you know your government has decreed that a Jesuit cannot enter the Massachusetts Bay Colony?" John and Thomas glanced at each other with surprised looks. "Oui, they are afraid we bring our pope to threaten your religious aristocracy. Do you not see how you are controlled by your clergy, how they conspire with what they consider the authority of 'The Lord?'"

John and Thomas traded more looks, but neither had a response to offer. They acted a little defeated and fatigued or just tired of the conversation.

"So, gentlemen, I ask you, who is the greater manipulator?" Father Francois must have recognized the effect of his arguments and tried changing the conversation's tone to alter the mood. "But let us not spoil our dinner trying to solve le grand dilemma in one evening. It will be up to others who follow to sort this all out someday. Young men like you, Elias, and your children! Are you ready for that challenge?" Elias had not been listening well as he fought off sleep while struggling to stay alert during the talking. He just shrugged his shoulders.

"Come, gentlemen, will you join me for a smoke and maybe brandy?"

A little lethargic after the big meal, the men eased toward the library to appease their host with their fatigue almost complete.

"Father Louis, I wish there were some way I could thank you for saving my life."

"God saved you, Mr. Sawyer. I was only his instrument."

"That was quite a trick, Father. How did you know you could frighten the natives enough to stop?"

"Not a trick, Mr. Sawyer. The natives call us 'Manitos.' It means 'other than human.' Look, my friends, men are the same everywhere. We are all afraid of the unknown. Life is a mystery, no? What we do not understand, we fear. And superstition, gentlemen, may be the most powerful force of all."

"That's why we need priests." John laughed.

"And ministers," replied Father Francois. Seriously, you English have seen how fear and superstition can infect men's souls. We know of your recent burning of witches not — all done in the name of God, no?"

"That's something we don't like to talk about," said John. "People would like to forget." When conversation shifted to home, exhaustion and the big meal combined, and Elias, his father and John began to struggle to stay awake.

"I think we'd better get to bed," said Thomas. "This has been quite an adventure, Father Louis, and the meal was wonderful, but now we want to head home. We are tired, but with some rest, we will be ready to start back, right, John?

"A few days should do it," John replied. "We'll just need

some provisions and a guide. And a few muskets would be good to keep those devils away."

In good time. Tomorrow you will meet with the governor, and everything will be worked out. For now, rest and be comfortable you are in God's hands."

THIRTEEN

DURING THE NEXT two days, small groups of curious Indians eased close to the prisoners' wigwam for a look at the new captives. Elias met several braves about his age who acted friendly, and he was surprised when one pointed at his chest.

"Lazar." Then with more pointing, it was obvious he was offering an invitation to go with him and a few others. Elias was ready to get out of the smoky, dark hut and eager as the young braves led him through the village. They stopped at the edge of a clearing beyond sight of the main settlement where a larger group of boys was waiting, squatting on their haunches in a semicircle. When Elias and his escorts approached, a gruff-looking brave stood to introduce himself.

"I Atonwa Aronhowonen! Great Sky!"

Atonwa stepped closer and stood as if to confront Elias in front of the group. The brave was about Elias's size and build with black tattoos under each eye that made his face look angry. Although the air was cold, Atonwa wore leggings with only a vest exposing his arms and bare chest. His head was shaved on one side, and Elias spotted the shine of a fat, white bone handle of a knife attached to his belt. He strode closer while spitting rough words before he stopped, his face close to Elias's. Atonwa turned to address his group, obviously mocking Elias, while the others laughed. Then, without warning, the Indian whirled back and with his momentum, muscled a savage, surprise punch, catching Elias on the side of his cheek.

Elias fell into the dirt, stunned, his head spinning, his hands catching his fall and stinging from the scrape of the stiff, frozen ground. He struggled on the edge of consciousness as the delighted howls of the boys filled his senses. His instinct made him roll over, pull his legs under himself and try to stand.

With words Elias could not understand, Atonwa boasted while he moved closer, waving his arms with exaggerated gesturing in what could only be a challenge. Elias had wrestled with his older brothers as a boy, but never really fought — never a real fight. He was confused, but there was no time or mistaking when the braves, now shouting and clapping, surrounded him and Atonwa. There could be no escaping.

Atonwa moved confidently, obviously secure in his place as leader of his group. He stepped in closer and swung again. Although still stunned from the punch, Elias was ready and ducked. As he did, and the whoosh of Atonwa's arm swung over him, he slipped up from under, driving with all the strength he could muster straight into the brave's body, toppling him to the ground. With grunts and angry mutterings, they clung to each other before Atonwa rolled over on top and began to punch, the first blow landing against Elias's eye before a flurry of others.

Excited screams erupted from the circle of spectators. Elias tried to protect his face, and with his best effort, pushed Atonwa off to the side. Then, with his senses clearing, he scrambled to his feet. The two combatants paused poised several feet apart, measuring each other. When Atonwa charged again, Elias met his rush, locking arms. Atonwa was not as strong as Elias had first thought, and a little soft too. As they grappled, Elias followed his instinct, dropping to one knee to wrap his arms around Atonwa's legs. Then he lifted and dropped his opponent to his back and began his own attack.

As Elias punched, the braves laughed and howled, clearly enjoying the battle while encouraging Atonwa. Elias pushed his advantage until his back exploded with sharp pain when one of the other braves piled into him, pushing him to the ground. Then Atonwa was on him again. But this time Elias was quick enough to slip free and sensed his attacker was not the same. Gone was the confident bluster from the beginning of the fight. With his chest heaving, Atonwa gasped for air, bent over, bracing himself with his hands on his knees, his breath laboring. Instead of another attack, Atonwa began to taunt Elias, his words an attempt to intimidate. But Elias sensed the advantage, and since his opponent was finished fighting, at least for now, Elias stepped forward closing the ground between them, this time with his own bluster.

"You're not as tough as you thought, are you?" Elias yelled as if trying to maintain his confidence. "Any time you want to dance again, just let me know. Next time when no one else is around!" The fight disintegrated into a shouting match as the others joined in the jeering. But Elias began to feel victorious, so he turned his hands with palms up, gesturing, bluffing, inviting Atonwa to come closer.

"Come on," he taunted with his fingers moving as if to coax. "Want some more?"

Instead of advancing, Atonwa's attention flirted to his laughing friends. Then he reached to his belt. The circle grew quiet when he pulled a long knife from its scabbard. He brandished the blade in front of his face with a twisting threat and two deliberate, confident steps forward.

But he stopped, and the fight ended with a shrill yell.

"Atonwa!"

Every boy cowered, including Atonwa, as the angry-sounding voice yelled again. It belonged to an Indian woman charging the group, swinging a three-foot-long branch. Elias stood still and surprised as the young braves scattered, including Atonwa, each wilting with the onslaught of the woman. She was covered in buckskin, her long brown hair flowing behind as she ran toward them. *What kind of power did this woman possess,* Elias wondered, amazed at what he was witnessing. After watching the group disperse, the woman held Elias's stare for a moment before turning away without a word to begin a determined walk back toward the village.

Elias touched near his eye, careful not to make it hurt more. His nose had dripped blood onto the front of his shirt, and when he touched the lump near his left eye, it had already swollen shut. His hands stung with tiny bits of dirt that had broken his skin. As he made his way back to the wigwam, he replayed the fight, what he should have done differently, but mostly wondered about what he would have done about that knife.

His clothes were dirty with a long tear on a shirtsleeve, and when he slipped inside, John and his father were alarmed.

"Elias! My God, what happened, Son?"

John grabbed Elias's shoulders and held him for a closer look. "Are you all right?"

"Yes, I think so — might look worse than it is. One of my new friends wanted to get better acquainted, that's all." The two adults traded glances as his father turned Elias's chin for a better look at his eye.

"Let's get some cold water on that."

"What happened?" asked John. "Who attacked you? How many were they?"

"One of the braves — Atonwa's his name."

They sat close while Elias recounted the story, with both adults remaining quiet, listening to every detail and description of the fight. Finally, John pressed his hands onto his thighs and stood with an angry-sounding grunt.

"If it were not for the French, these savages would sooner cut our throats than look at us. This just shows how careful we still need to be."

"You're right John. From now on, we stay together! Always!" Thomas was angry, acting more concerned than Elias could ever remember.

"And trust no one!" added John. "I'm afraid with these devils we'll need to watch our backs all the time. This buck sounds like a mean one."

"He's jealous, all right," said Thomas. "It's a sure sign; you've never bothered him. He must want to show you and his friends he's boss — like a cock rooster. He thinks you're going to threaten his position."

"Your father's right," said John. "Jealousy might be the strongest feeling. Drives men to kill."

"From now on none of us goes anywhere alone, understand?" Elias's father paused for agreement. "We may have been fortunate this far, but you're right, John. No telling what these animals might do if they get the chance."

It was unnecessary advice; Elias planned to be ready next time. Even though his body hurt, and he must look defeated, he was alright. The fight had done something unexpected — revealing strength he did not know he had, along with growing confidence that neither Atonwa nor anyone else could damage. His eye was swollen shut, his scraped hands stung, but his shame was gone.

Elias had to admit, he was still worried about what Atonwa might do next. And he could not help thinking about that knife.

FOURTEEN

G OVERNOR VAUDREUIL'S RESIDENCE was the grandest
building Elias had ever seen.

"Father," he asked, "how would this look in Lancaster?"

The building rose five stories with at least twenty-five
glassed windows in front stretching across each floor. The walls
were stone blocks, each cut to fit perfectly. Rock patios flanked
both sides. Elias thought many families could live protected
inside as they did at home. *Home.* It was so far away, and for a
moment, he thought of his mother and one of her big hugs in
front of the fire. He was hoping it would not be long now —
maybe they could get back before the heavy winter snow began.

An Indian servant greeted the three men at the door, inviting them to sit in the parlor to wait. The chairs were large and
cushioned. On the hall wall entering the room was a large
mirror, almost floor length. Elias's father noticed first.

"Come here, Elias. You too John. Look!" When the three
prisoners considered the mirror, they were quiet — until John
laughed.

"Who are these beggars?"

"Whoever they are," said Thomas, "they could sure use some new clothes. And a bath!"

Their skin was unwashed and pallid; their shirts and pants hung loosely from their frames with their skin pulled tight against the bones of their faces. Elias noticed darker hair on his chin and brushed his cheek with the back of his hand, enjoying the rough feel. He did not much mind his appearance. Others had commented on his growth spurt, but this was the first time he had a good look in a mirror. They had walked for over a month, and one boot had lost its heel. His pants were ripped in several places with brown dirt splotches. His shirt was not much better, with one sleeve torn during the fight with Atonwa. His dark brown hair rested on wide shoulders. He was taller than John, or his father and most of the men at home. He knew his voice was still a boy's, but he was beginning to feel more confident when he had something to say. John looked as ragged, but he continued to make them all laugh.

"We better send home to have the women make us some fresh clothes — and a size smaller!" The governor did not make them wait long.

"Gentlemen!" an Indian aide announced. "Governor Vaudreuil will see you now!"

They walked through a long hall with more portraits adorning the walls before turning into a large inner office. Another aide, an older-looking French man, introduced their host with an elaborate sweep of his hand.

"I am pleased to present, the Gouverneur General de Quebec, Philippe de Rigaud Vaudreuil."

Governor Vaudreuil circled to greet them from behind an

enormous, dark wooden desk. He was a round man, shorter than his three visitors. His black coat jacket covered a bright white shirt, striped with a thin black tie. His pants stopped at the knee with white stockings descending to black shoes. His hair was black with a bit of gray over his ears, the only facial hair a thin mustache with edges drooping on each end.

"You must be the Mr. Sawyer I am hearing about? And who is this?" The governor was gushing.

"This is my son, Elias, and this is our friend, John Bigelow. We are from the south — Lancaster and Marlborough — in Massachusetts Bay Colony."

"Well, welcome to New France! I am glad you are safe. I hope our native friends were not, how you say, too rough with you?"

"There were times," replied John, "but we hope that's all behind us."

"Yes, they can be enthusiastic. And how about you, young man? How are you enjoying your adventure?" *Adventure.* Elias, for the first time since the capture, understood. He had not considered this an adventure, but the governor had stirred a new feeling. *It had been an adventure.* He was eager now to return home with a story he could relish telling his family and friends. He imagined others his age crowding near, urging him on, and hungry for every detail. Aside from his blisters, the cold, hungry nights and his father's close call, they had survived the ordeal.

"It's been very different — but exciting too." Elias's next comment was a surprise to everyone. "They seem happy — the people, I mean. The Indians. They seem to be enjoying their lives."

"You have a very perceptive young man here, Mr. Sawyer. The Indians are happy. You must remember, Elias, they have been living this way from the beginning. Their culture is much older than yours or mine. Granted, they have some strange ways, and many things that cause me to wonder — their customs, their God. I would not want to say this in front of my Jesuit associates, but the Indians' concept of God does make a lot of sense. I mean, Native Americans see God everywhere. Sounds primitive, no?

The men waited for more, and the governor continued as if he had been waiting for an audience.

"They see spirit in everything — the animals, the deer, the bear, trees, forest, the waterfall. Everything — even rocks. All part of one!" Governor Vaudreuil signaled an aide who brought glasses half-filled with red wine. "They teach their children some interesting things. They say the spirit is inside each of them, easily reached when they sit quietly, appreciating the beauty around them."

"That's well said, Governor," said Thomas. "It certainly is an appealing idea. And the land, it is beautiful."

"Someday, it may be all European," John said. "It's God's will."

"Well, not entirely, my new friend. That may be true for the English land, but not for New France. You see, the natives are our brethren, and the English, well, not so much. Which leads me to the reason you are here."

"Yes, Governor," said John. "We have been waiting to get to that. We are all anxious to head home."

"Oh course, of course. I will get right to the point then." The governor moved back behind his desk and sat while speaking in a suddenly more formal fashion. "Let me be frank, Gentlemen. Do you suspect you may not have been a random choice for le removal?"

"I did wonder about that," replied John.

"You, John, are a carpenter, no? And you, Mr. Sawyer, a miller, correct?"

"What are you getting at?" asked Mr. Sawyer. "You mean we were selected?"

"Mr. Sawyer, you can draw conclusions as to your circumstances. Let us just say your skills are a match for certain needs we have in New France. You can be a great help to us."

"You ordered this?" snapped John. "You set these devils upon us?"

An aide appeared in the doorway, but the Governor dismissed him with a casual gesture and remained silent as if waiting for the tension to ease a bit before he responded.

"Gentlemen," he began in a patient-sounding tone. "Let me explain some things, if I may, about the reality of our North American conflict. The French were here long before the English. You know that is true, no? And we intend to continue building a new country. But now you English have arrived. First a few, but your settlers come by the thousands, each hungry for land, claiming everything for themselves. Our new King, Louis XIV, has seen this and decreed we will prevent your expansion, containing you east of your Alleghany Mountains. The land south from the Great Lakes through the Ohio, and Missouri River Valleys and down the Mississippi River will always remain the property of France."

"Do you really think you can accomplish that?" asked Thomas.

"You see, we are building our forts as we speak — at Ticonderoga — soon at Detroit and Pontiac. And there will be many others." The governor paused, lifting his glass to finish his wine. "There is another important factor to consider. You see, the Indians hate the English. You have taken their land with trickery and greed, killed their women and children, burned their villages. You can no longer disguise your intentions. So, you see, Gentlemen, the French and the Indian, we have become allies because we must — the necessity of survival."

"That doesn't give you the right to murder and kidnap," snapped John.

"You will come to better understand the circumstances concerning your involvement in our endeavors, Mr. Bigelow. For now, we must not talk about the past. Instead, let us discuss what is, and what will be, n'est-ce pas?"

An aide returned to the room and offered the wine bottle near John's glass.

"More wine?"

"Yes, I will have a little more," John said. "It has been a long time."

"Governor," Mr. Sawyer pressed. "Why don't you just spell it out for us?"

"Certainement," Mr. Sawyer. As you say, we should go to the point. Soon we will arrange your purchase from the Indians. The final amount is not important for our discussion today. When the transaction is complete, then you will begin to work for us."

"Work for you!" barked John. "Doing what?"

"We would like you to build us a mill. You and Mr. Sawyer. And, of course, Elias as well."

The three prisoners traded surprised looks.

"You, John, are le carpenter, n'est-ce pas? You will build le mill. Then you can return to your home. Simple as that."

"And if we don't agree?" John's voice was rising as if the wine might have begun to affect him.

"Well, I don't think that would be wise. Mr. Bigelow. If, as you say, I was in the shoes of yours, I would want to get started. You see, the sooner you complete the job, the sooner you can leave for home." The governor waited as if to let that idea sink in, then turned and gestured for the attention of a servant before returning to his guests. "Gentlemen, in this matter, I don't see where you have much of a choice."

Elias looked at his father and then John, not sure how they would respond to the ultimatum. He wanted to go home now. His father looked at each of them, and then with the calm Elias expected, finally addressed the governor.

"So, where do you want it, Governor — your new mill?"

"Ah, good then!" The governor rose with an excited clap of his hands. "We have agreed! Let us get started!" With that, he made another slight gesture before an attendant produced a scroll. When another two waiters cleared the end of the table, the governor rolled out a map.

"Where it should be built is a good question, but that we leave up to you, Mr. Sawyer. That is why you are here — for how you say — your expertise. We have plenty of rivers from which to choose, wouldn't you say?"

"Yes, Governor." Thomas studied the elaborate, detailed map. The rivers were marked clearly on the map, each feeding north or south into the Saint Lawrence River. "We could make you a beautiful mill." He glanced to John. "Right John?"

John was quiet, he too studying the map.

"Would it be your first in Canada?" he asked.

"Oui!" exclaimed the governor. "And you will be the one to build it! Then we will build many. Think of it! You, Englishmen, will leave your name in history — on the first mill in New France!"

"How do we know what you say will happen?" John asked.

"Ah," the governor laughed. "You are asking how you know if you can trust me? Well, I am afraid you cannot be entirely sure. You see, Mr. Bigelow, that comes along with being detained, n'est-ce pas?"

John held his tongue; instead, he threw his head back and drained the last of his wine. When he placed the empty glass on the table, with an exaggerated, deliberate manner, he looked defeated.

"Although your choices are not what you might like, considering the ill will surrounding you from others, would you think it a bad bargain? You will be fed well and kept safe. We will even pay you for your work. And best of all, you and your family will see each other again. It's not every captive from your land that can say as much." The governor watched for the reactions he must have expected. "I should also mention, Elias will have an amazing story to tell his children and grandchildren one day. What do you say, Elias? Are you ready to help make history in New France?"

After a quick look at his father, Elias shrugged an answer. "I don't know, I guess so."

"It's settled then! Shall we get started, Mr. Sawyer? How about you, Mr. Bigelow — are you ready to get to work?"

John and Thomas shared a look, and then Mr. Sawyer addressed Elias.

"Well Son, it wasn't how we'd planned to spend the winter, but it looks like now we are going to learn something about life in the north. The Lord moves in mysterious ways, Governor, his wonders to perform. It looks like he has chosen us for a special task."

"Wonderful! If we are all in agreement, I will speak with Chief Pukeewis, and you can begin your work immediately. The first step will be to choose a site. My staff will provide a guide, and you can look over our options. Just think, Elias, someday the world will know about three brave men who traveled to Canada from Lancaster to help build a new country!"

FIFTEEN

IN THE MORNING, Lazar, whom Elias remembered, along with two others, arrived at the wigwam. They provided beaver skins for the captives to cover their shoulders and chests. With a warm smile, Lazar introduced himself and his companions, Joachim, and a woman he called Marguerite. The woman's body was snuggled in a deerskin covering that draped over moccasin leggings, the same as all other Indian women Elias had seen. He had not noticed anything unusual and thought Marguerite could be the same age as his older sister, approaching middle years. But when the guide dropped her hood, Elias was surprised when he recognized her — the same woman who had interrupted the fight a few days before.

Elias smiled as if to thank her, but she acted as if nothing had happened. Then she surprised Elias again — when she spoke.

"Hello, your name is Elias, I've learned. That eye looks painful."

Elias's mouth dropped open, and he could not respond.

"Hello, Thomas Sawyer," she continued. "And you are John Bigelow, n'est-ce pas? Elias and I have already met."

Elias found his voice.

"You talk! English, I mean. You speak! You talk English!"

"Yes, Abenaki and French as well. I speak several languages. I am Marguerite, from the Missiquoi tribe — wife of Gray Elk. I am the mother of three: Parquette, Malgelit and my youngest, Malian." Elias was surprised at Marguerite's fluency and delighted to hear English without struggling to understand the meaning of Indian words.

"How did you learn to speak English so well?" John asked.

"I was born English, captured when I was seven. My brother Stephen, as well. He was four. Francais, they sent me to help today. They often use me when the English traders sneak up from Al-ban-ee to trade for furs with guns and English clothes. I interpret. Now I am to help you with your project — to find your mill site." Elias could not help wondering how the woman had become an Indian. "If you are to succeed," she continued, "we will need to communicate."

As they walked, Thomas explained what they were looking for.

"We don't want too big of a river; too much water is not good. We need a more moderate volume, with a good current that does not go too low in summer. We will build a canal to divert a flow to power the mill. We passed several on our journey north. I'm sure we can find something that will work close by."

"We can look as long as you like," Marguerite said. "But we should hurry. Snows will come soon." They had seen a few flurries before arriving in Quebec, but the Sawyers and John knew what real snow was like at home, how paralyzing it could be with drifts piled higher than the windows. They did not want to try trudging through woods after storms that could drop over two feet. Already, it was so cold their noses stung, and breath smoked out in front of their faces as they followed the trails alongside the rivers.

"My heavens," said Thomas, "how I would love to have these rivers and streams around Lancaster! We would build a string of sawmills. The size and fall of water are perfect to turn the wheels. I'm surprised they haven't built any mills yet."

The quiet woods smelled of pine, and the trails they followed were well worn. One path crested a hill where the woods opened at an overhang of rocks high above a valley revealing a vista that rivaled any at home. They discovered another beautiful spot at the falls where the Saint Louis River met with what Marguerite called the Trois Rivers. At many places, the slope of land created a roaring rapid, while other sections of a river fell more than fifty feet with an occasional waterfall.

For the next several days, they evaluated many potential sites. Some days Margurite joined them while others they followed a new guide. Each night they returned first to Marguerite's wigwam where she cooked for them and her family. While they ate, Marguerite interpreted for her husband, Gray Elk, who had many questions for the first white men he had met.

"How did you travel to this land? How many suns? How many white men are in your land? What do they do each day? What do they eat?"

The prisoners had plenty of questions for Gray Elk as well

— about his tribe and their elders, their customs, when did they marry? How did they teach their children?

"Marguerite, ask your husband why they attack English settlers?" John wanted to know why they could not live together in peace. Elias was surprised at how well Marguerite spoke English after so long. She said she was remembering more words as they spent time together. Although she mentioned her parents once, she said her memory was weak, and now her children and husband were her only life. For Elias, there was no doubt — she was all Indian.

As their stomachs filled with moose meat and corn, and their reserve evaporated, they relaxed, enjoying each other's company. Then John asked Marguerite a bold question — one Elias had wondered too.

"Why did you stay here and marry? Did the Indians force you?"

"No. I had a choice. I spent the first two years secluded after my capture. My father was a minister, and he came to ransom me, but the tribal elders prevented it. They protected and cared well for me. The Jesuits taught me Latin and how to be a Catholic, then baptized me with my Catholic name. When I was older, I was offered a choice to leave, but by then I liked it here." After more questions from the men about kidnapping white settlers, Marguerite explained how taking children from other tribes was an Indian tradition.

"There are many captives here. They treat us like their own and do not see it as wrong. Children adapt easily to this life. After a short time, like me, most do not want to return to the white man's world. For the young, Indian life is exciting."

Elias wondered about other things, but he let Marguerite

continue. There would be plenty of time for his questions.

"Everything we need is here — the woods, the rivers, beaver, deer. And we have each other. My children are happy and growing in the ways of our People."

"Are there more — other white children living here with the Indians?"

"Oh, yes, John, many like me — hundreds, I'm told. I often see a pale face and wonder about their story — where they came from. I know of a tribe with two white chiefs — twin brothers captured as children. They just never left."

"What about their families?" asked Thomas.

"They tried sending messengers and offers, but the boys wouldn't return. Indian life is a delight for children — especially for boys. Many young die, before ten snows, most from white man's disease. Myself, I have lost four babies. Our nation struggles to survive. The men need to bring more children to keep our tribe alive. Our women cannot make babies fast enough."

Elias was astonished at what Marguerite was explaining. When the conversations got deeper, Gray Elk struggled to understand Marguerite's words, but when she took time to translate and encouraged him to participate, he joined in.

"Boys fish and hunt all day," he explained through Marguerite. "Fathers are busy with other things, so elders teach our young. Children spend time with grandparents — and each other. That is how they learn. That is the Indian way. Husbands hunt — go on raids. When the boy is ready, younger than you Elias, he becomes a full brave ready to leave home."

"They never work?" asked Thomas.

"In the Indian life," explained Marguerite, "the work is

done by women. We understand and accept that. A girl learns the ways from her mother: cooking, washing, gathering firewood, having babies, caring for families. And she runs the family when her man is away. A mother's word is the law — our husbands respect that. The People listen to our counsel in choosing tribal representatives. A few women have become sachem when their husbands died or, because of their wisdom, they were chosen by the tribal council."

During their time together at Marguerite's home, Elias grew familiar and closer to her children. He taught Malian and Malgelit white man's counting games and many English words. The teaching went both ways as Elias was learning Abenaki, and it was not long before he could converse with the young braves of the camp and form friendships. The young Indians did not seem threatened and took interest in Elias, eager to learn his words and ways, although some, like Atonwa, remained aloof.

One day, after almost two weeks, as they walked along a riverbank, Thomas stopped the group. He spread his arms.

"This is it! This is where we will build the mill. What's this river called?"

"It is the Iroquois." said Marguerite. "The French named it Chambly." Thomas pointed to a rock, about a two-foot square.

"We need stones like this one, for the foundation. We're going to need plenty." When he pushed at it, Elias joined, but it did not budge.

"Ground's frozen solid. A little smaller would be better, anyway — not too heavy and easier to move. We need some sleds too — and oxen. You can get oxen, right?"

"Yes," said Marguerite, "the French have many. They will

provide whatever you need."

"Well, if you can get that started, they can begin gathering stones as soon as they like. But it's too late this year. The ground is frozen solid; it will be snowing soon. You get a bit of snow here, right?" They all laughed when Marguerite held her arms out at shoulder height and said,

"Only a little."

"There's plenty of stones like this around," said Mr. Sawyer, "but we want them as square as possible. Show them this one; we want them just like this."

John said he would start on the plans right away.

"How big do you think, Thomas?"

"Don't know quite yet. We can work on the design. We have plenty of time — we can make a big one if we want. The French can help get the trees cut. We will not have to go far for those either. Take your pick!"

Marguerite asked, "What will it look like?"

Thomas took a stick, cleared the leaves and tried to scratch out the design, but the dirt was solid. He explained how they would build the foundation to straddle the brook that dumped into the river.

"John will design an enclosure to rest on top of the stones. Each log will be notched to fit into the adjoining cross piece. There will be openings for light and a fireplace for heat." John suggested they shape the logs inside a warm enclosure and then drag them to the site in the spring.

"Going to take some time to build this right," John said. "I wonder what they have for tools."

"Just tell them what you need," said Marguerite. "Governor Vaudreuil can come up with most anything. He'll even send to

France for whatever he needs."

"Should we insist on nails, John?"

"We won't need many, Thomas. We could use a few though."

"How long will it take to build?" Elias asked.

John looked at Thomas and then addressed Elias.

"Well, Elias, if things go right, we should be on our way home by late summer."

Late summer. Such a long time. Elias had hoped for sooner than that. As the adults' conversation drifted to the background, Elias thought about home, and when his fingers touched the edges of his swollen eye, he thought about Atonwa.

SIXTEEN

W ITH HIS FATHER and John busy planning the mill, there
was not much for Elias to do all day, so when Joachim
and Lazar, along with a few other braves called from outside
the wigwam, he invited them in, hesitating only until he was
sure Atonwa was not with them.

"You come, Elias," urged Joachim. "To hunt with us?" He
did not have to coax; Elias was ready to go anywhere. As the
days passed, Elias had begun to feel more comfortable with the
Indian boys. They accepted him, and Lazar confided it had a lot
to do with his unexpected courage in his fight with Atonwa.

They headed out: Joachim, Azon, Wematin, Awasos, Francois and Lazar. Azon and Francois carried bows while the
others had muskets. They walked along a riverbank in silence
for hours before the river slowed into a languid current. With
silent signals, the boys fanned out around a place that offered a
low bank and good access to the water's edge. With palms
turned down, Joachim gestured to indicate they would wait for

the deer to arrive. Elias got the message — be quiet and still.

They had provided Elias a bow and a few arrows, but he had never used one, so he was not expecting to hit anything. Dusk came, but no deer. He was cramped and thinking of the warm fire while noticing none of the braves had moved. When darkness closed around them, Elias thought the braves would give up and pick their way back. But when that did not happen, he grew more uncomfortable — and sleepy. Sometime later, gunshots echoed, the sound jarring Elias from a dream. With the boys' shouting, he lurched from his hiding place to find what they had hit. One deer lay squirming with two arrows — one in its side and one in its neck. Nearby, another deer lay dead from a single bullet. Joachim slit the struggling deer's throat before Azon and Lazar tied its hind legs and looped the rawhide line over a tree. While they hoisted the animal to shoulder height, Francois and Awasos did the same with the second deer.

Joachim plunged his knife into the deer's neck under the jaw, ripping the carcass open down to the genitals. After gutting both animals, they slung each on a carrying rack between two braves for the return home. Elias grabbed one end of a pole — he wanted to contribute something.

Although the trip home was difficult in the dark, the night was lit by a three-quarter moon helping the hunters find their way. Elias's shoulder burned from supporting the weight of the carcass, but it was a delicious sting, a small price to pay for being invited on the hunt. As he tripped and stumbled over the rough spots in the trail, he was happy with the new friendships and the effort, unlike working at home. This labor was exhilarating. He could not wait for the shouts of praise they would hear at camp and hoped his father and John would wake to see them. If not, he would surprise them with fresh meat for their breakfast.

When they got back, sisters and mothers greeted them with hugs and excited squeals. Women called names of sons and brothers as they emerged from the wigwams, celebrating what the boys had done. Gray Elk embraced Elias.

"Good hunt, Elias. You learn well!"

"Anybody can carry the kill, Gray Elk. I need to learn to shoot a bow!"

"We do that. I show. You show English words!"

Elias rushed to wake John and his father to tell them about the hunt.

"We waited at the place they said the deer would come, near the water's edge. We got there late and stayed all night until a herd came to drink. You should have seen the braves, Father! They had the deer dressed in no time — like second nature. Must have been doing it since they were small."

John said he was impressed they had taken Elias along.

"You will be quite the expert before we get home, Elias. You'll be able to teach the home folks a few things. Now, I'll be looking forward to a big meal at Marguerite's!"

Elias's father explained how the Indians once hunted around Lancaster when he was a young boy.

"They didn't stalk the deer. The braves burned several meadows each year to keep the brush from growing, so the grass grew high. The hunters hid nearby waiting for the deer to come for the soft grass. When the white man arrived, farmers had ready-made hay fields and pastures."

John offered the names: "Springfield, Hatfield, Deerfield —

Greenfield and Pittsfield too, in the Connecticut Valley."

"I'm surprised how many muskets I see, Father. Most families have at least one."

"It's not a crime to sell Indians weapons here — not like at home."

"Beaver skins make the law here," said John. "English muskets demand a big price in pelts. That is just the way it is. Besides, the French know Indians need to live too."

"The French are not as worried about it as the folks back home," said Thomas. "It's too bad we didn't learn that too. Maybe then we wouldn't have to be afraid all the time."

******

DESPITE THE PLANNING of the mill, there were quiet times during lonely nights when longing for home gnawed at them. John and Elias's father talked of their wives and families while Elias talked about his mother and brothers and sisters. One night in the wigwam, Thomas noticed John was quiet — writing.

"What are you writing?" When John did not look up or answer, Thomas persisted.

"And where did you get the paper and ink?"

"Kind of nosey, aren't you?" John gave Thomas a long stare, but it was not an angry one. "If you must know, Marguerite got it for me — to write Jerusha. This letter will make her feel a lot better. I want her to be patient until I return in the summer."

"You mean you don't want her getting too lonely. You sure don't want to leave a young wife alone too long. Be sure to tell her how much you miss her."

"Hush, Thomas. She would never think of another man, not after I smiled at her."

"Maybe so, John, but that letter better get to her quick. Tell her how much you miss her." Elias giggled as his father kept goading John. "Problem is, it may never arrive. Could go to Arcadia or Albany first. We might even get back before your letter!"

"Thomas, what do you know about it, you old plow horse? What are you, seventy — eighty?"

"Almost."

"Right," laughed John. "Your Hannah is likely glad to have you out of the house." They teased until John became more serious. "I think of Jerusha every night, imagining her arms around me while I hold her in the dark. I figure I must have done some transgression, and this is God's cruel punishment. I'm certain of it!"

"If it makes you feel better, John. I've wondered about that myself."

"I hoped a letter might help me with this ordeal. I learned that mail goes between the colony and here, even if it does take a while to get where it is supposed to. Can you imagine how this will be received in Lancaster? They must think we're all dead!"

"Be sure to tell her my father and I are all right too."

"Don't worry, Elias. I'll tell her to nail this on the door for everyone to see." John laughed at his joke. "That should keep the young bucks from sniffing around!"

"Yeah, John, it's been a long time. They might be circling your nest by now."

The three howled at Thomas's joke, but Elias could tell the

laughter masked their ache for home, while suspecting the men's thoughts of their wives must have an especially cruel sting.

SEVENTEEN

S NOW CAME, FALLING regularly, piling up over four feet, drifting high over their heads. Moving about required following the trampled paths between wigwams. The cold was more severe than Elias had experienced, and since there was nothing to do outside until spring, their days were spent inside near the fire, eating, talking or sleeping. Thomas and John even became friendly with a few adult Indian males who were doing the same.

As for building the mill, Thomas had been right — the ground was frozen solid and would not give up the stones they needed. As the moons changed, and the long winter dragged, the daylight was brief, and the snow piled in feet. The only activity was hunting. Building a mill and the natives' raiding ventures were put on hold until the return of milder weather.

John and Thomas spent hours making plans. Marguerite was right — Governor Vaudreuil proved eager to deliver everything they requested with tools, writing paper, pencils and parchment to map their designs. Supply transports from France came regularly, and Governor Vaudreuil included all their requests in his correspondence.

Word was out about the project, and there was excitement outside their wigwam. John and Thomas had thrown themselves into the project, which helped keep the prospect of leaving for home out of their minds. One look outside the wigwam at the snow that drifted in unexpected ways, the frozen ponds, whitened treetops and howling wind that shook the hut was enough to remind them that they were not going far anytime soon. The best thing to do was prepare well and be ready with the spring thaw. The quicker the project was completed, the quicker their departure would be.

"Let's not make it too big, Thomas — get it done and get on the way home. Canada is not to my liking when I have a warm English bed and dinner rolls waiting for me."

"Don't worry about that, John. This will be the fastest mill ever built!" After they had laughed, Thomas continued. "But if we are going to build this, let's make it something we can all be proud of."

While Thomas and John planned, they hardly saw Elias. He spent most of his time with Marguerite's family. He had become like a big brother to her children, and unlike the Indian men, he would offer to help with the chores. He trudged through deep snow to reach new places to find the best firewood. Lazar had even provided him a pair of snowshoes to help him get around. And said, "You're not going far without these!" They were simple footgear, made from two hickory branches bent together, fastened in a half-circle with several cross pieces and a fastener for each foot. Elias could walk across the top of the snow without pressing through to his hips. When he built a load, he would struggle back to drop the pile outside Marguerite's wigwam. Other boys mocked him for doing woman's work, but Elias could tell how much Marguerite appreciated his effort. After all, he thought, an English man can always be counted on to provide a warm home.

On one return, Elias suddenly forgot the cold wind and weight of the firewood. He was surprised in front of another family's hut when the flap opened, and a girl stepped out. He guessed she was not much younger than he. She wore a sparkling white deerskin dress which covered her body halfway down her thighs. Her long black hair hung to her buttocks, held loosely by what looked like a fishbone clasp. Her skin was almond-colored, like others in the tribe, her face bright with high cheekbones. Holding her hand was a younger girl, eight or nine, he guessed, the older one leading her gently as they moved away.

While Elias's eyes burned their backs, the two girls walked toward the main village. When they had traveled a good piece, the younger girl, who must have sensed Elias's stare, turned her head to look backward. She locked eyes with his before snapping her head back forward with an embarrassed jerk.

Elias had not realized he had watched for such a long time. The younger girl had noticed him while the older continued as if he was not there. He had sometimes noticed attractive girls at home, dressed in their bonnets and finest clothes for Sunday meeting. His friends had compared notes on favorites — whose bodies hinted from under their dresses. He had noticed the way some girls moved as they slid into a church pew or walked down the front steps of the church. In Lancaster, young folks looked to marry as soon as they could, but since it was still several years away for him, he did not give it much thought. Boys still made jokes about who would be the best mate, but it was only big talk. Few were brave enough to talk to a girl who was not a sister. The same could be said of the girls who were careful to keep their gazes away from an awkward boy with a squeaking voice and fuzz on his chin.

Elias's eyes followed the Abenaki girls until they disappeared into the jumble of huts deeper in the village. *I wonder who that is.* During his time spent with the village boys, they had mentioned girls but never someone like her. *It's odd I've never noticed her before.* If she was the sister of one of his new friends, she should have been at one of the fires with a celebration or meal. Her bright covering was unusual too. Everything about her was special. *I will ask Marguerite; she will know.* He hurried to get back to her wigwam and his new family. The children would be waiting, and Marguerite would have something good cooking in the pot. But for once, he was less interested in food.

EIGHTEEN

E LIAS WASTED LITTLE time with Marguerite to get what he wanted.

"That must be Owaissa," Marguerite said. "She is the daughter of Ottowa — the brother of Chief Pukeewis."

"What does it mean?" Elias asked.

"Mean? What, her name? Does every native name need to mean something?"

"No. I mean, I just thought…"

"Many call her Bluebird."

"How is it I've never seen her before in the village with the others?"

"Because she spends most of her time at the Jesuit school — The Sisters of the Congregation at Ville Marie. Pukeewis's relatives and a select few learn French there — and the Catholic religion. I'm told she has been taught the same as those in the best French university, like a French princess — Latin and Greek — and how to write."

"How old is she?" Elias asked.

Marguerite paused, studying Elias who was trying to appear casual with his questions while he broke pieces from the pine branches he had gathered. Marguerite was not fooled.

"Not old enough for you, my young Englishman. Her father will make sure of that." But Elias had the information he wanted and changed the subject.

"Lazar and Joachim and some of the others are ice fishing, and I'm joining them. Would you like me to take Black Turtle?"

"He can go if he wants but be careful with him. Bundle him up good; he gets cold easily." "Don't worry; we'll make a big fire and keep him warm."

Elias and Black Turtle joined the others on the ice. They re-opened two fishing holes that had been cut the day before by chopping with a long spear with a sharp rock fastened to the end. When they had reached the water's surface, Joachim baited a hook made from a broken bone and slipped a line into the hole, repeating the process at several more holes. Joachim fastened the line to the handle of a knife that he stabbed into the ice. By lifting the line over a small branch that would wiggle, they could tell when the bait had been taken.

When they had the lines set, they joined others at a fire blazing near the center of the ice.

"Do you like fishing, Black Turtle?"

"I'm cold," he answered.

"Well, get closer to the fire. Here, have some of this bread your mother packed for us. That will make you feel warmer. We need to bring some nice bass home for dinner. That will make her happy."

"Are you going to help the others building your English mill?" asked Joachim.

"Yes, I know about mills; that is my work at home."

"Your work?" asked Joachim.

"Work — each day. In my country, everyone has work to do."

"You mean, like our women?"

"Well, yes. I mean no. Women have their work too — like taking care of the family and preparing meals — making clothes. They stay at the house. I go to the mill with my father." Lazar looked at Joachim and Wematin — then back to Elias.

"Don't you hunt?" asked Joachim.

"Yes, of course. But not all the time. Not like you. Some men hunt more than others. But we have crops to tend and hay to cut and animals to care for. That takes a lot of time."

"And you," Lazar asked, "do you do those things too?"

"No, I mean, sometimes I do. But mostly, I just work at the mill."

"So, you don't do those other things?"

"You see, Lazar, in my land, it's like this. A man has a job — his profession. It's what we call it. Some make shoes — others make plates and utensils — even guns. Blacksmiths do ironwork and horseshoeing. Tanners make skins. There are clothes makers, coachmen, sailors, ministers. Each man is known for what he does. Not like your people. We are different. We each have a special job."

"What do you do when you go to your mill?"

"We saw — and shave the logs into flat boards to build houses."

"You don't build houses like the French men, with stones?"

"Sometimes — only in the cities though. Where I live, we use the trees; we have plenty, to make the boards to make the houses — and churches and barns. People come from all over to buy boards or bring logs with their oxen for us to cut."

"And they give you trade things?" Lazar asked.

"Yes — and money."

The Indian boys listened as if trying to picture Elias's life. As the winter moved on, they spent many days together — fishing, and hunting and talking, coming to know each other like brothers. Elias had a few friends at home, but they were not as close as these had become and never shared like this — important topics, like life and death — mysteries. He slept at their wigwams, and they talked while eating meals with their parents, brothers and sisters, cousins and friends. Before long, there were not many secrets between them. However, Elias was holding some things back and not ready to mention Owaissa — at least not to his friends — not yet.

"I don't like that life," said Joachim after he had thought about it for a while. "I like the way of The People, the same as my father and his father and the fathers before. I am Wabanaki. Our ways have always been. I hunt and fish and will soon keep a woman. I would not want to live like you, with your special work to do each day for other men."

Lazar laughed. "Your dreams are too big, Joachim. You are too ugly and weak for a woman. What girl will want you?"

They all laughed and joined the teasing.

"Some moose cow might," laughed Wematin.

"Yeah," taunted Lazar. "A French cow who will lick your face each morning." The five boys held their sides as they laughed, and even Black Turtle understood the joke.

"Maybe you can marry it," the eight-year-old said. With the remark, the four older boys stopped to stare in surprise. Then Joachim grabbed the child and rolled him into the snow, landing on top of the squealing boy. Elias tackled Joachim, pushing him into the snow where they wrestled until their energy waned. When they had caught their breath, Joachim asked his friend.

"So, what about you, Elias? Do you have a woman picked out at your home?"

"Yeah," asked Lazar. "Are your young white women as fine as our maidens?"

"Better!" said Elias. "But I'm too young to worry about that. A few more years, maybe then."

"Do they have long black hair and dark eyes like Lilly?"

"How about Malian?" asked Joachim. "Beautiful like her?

"Some," answered Elias. "Better though." The boys laughed again.

"Don't get near Malian," said Joachim. "She's only fourteen. Her mother is a bear. She sees us looking, and she chases us away. She threw a hot coal at me one day!"

Their laughter was contagious with Black Turtle joining in, squealing and trying to outdo the older boys.

"Her father watches too," said Lazar. "He'd cut you up and use you for dog food!"

Their time together was not always spent laughing; they tested each other regularly. Throughout the winter and into spring, Lazar sprouted into a tall, strong man — slightly bigger than Elias. When the boys wrestled, measuring their strength against each other, Lazar was all Elias could handle, and he had to use all his tricks for advantage, but Lazar began to dominate.

"I am much French," he boasted, "small part Missisquois and small part Iroquois. My grandfather was trapper and mother the daughter of trapper and Ojibwas woman. I do not know what that makes me, but I do know this. I am better man than you full bloods all put together. I have more great parts!"

Joachim challenged Lazar. "Just because you're big like a moose, that doesn't make you any better. My grandfather told me most of us are mixed blood. He said trappers need company on cold nights and leave a trail. Many babies are born saying, "Oui, oui."

The other boys could not deny that Lazar was impressive, and his confidence was apparent. When spring came, he wore nothing but moccasins and the traditional breechcloth to cover his loins. He had shaved the sides of his head like a warrior with the remaining long hair trailing down his back. Across his biceps were beaded bands circling upper arms that had grown thicker than most. He had always been able to run faster and further than anyone, not just those his age, so Elias was not surprised when he heard Lazar talking about accompanying the older braves when they next went on raids south — into the Connecticut River Valley.

"Lazar will be a full brave before any of us," Joachim confided. "A great warrior someday — maybe even a chief. Grandmother says the elders have noticed him already."

Then one day Lazar came to share his great news.

"Grandfather says I am ready, Elias! I will be included to travel south — on the next raid."

"When?"

"Soon — with the new moon."

"What does that mean, Lazar?" growled Elias. "You're going savage to kill English?"

"No, Elias. I mean, only if they try to kill me. You do know the English soldiers kill our people — in the hundreds — even women and children. Someday you should listen to the stories before you call our people evil. We are just going for captives." Lazar did not seem finished trying to educate his friend; he was busy sharpening his knife — as if more concerned with that than talking. When he stopped sharpening, he returned his attention to Elias.

"My aunt lost her daughter last year to white man's measles; she cries for another little girl to love. And we need white man's muskets more than ever. Without guns, other tribes will slaughter us and take our women." Lazar must have seen his words were having a sobering effect on his friend, so he broke the mood.

"Maybe we could capture another Elias."

"That will not happen, my Indian friend. Are you sure your mother will let you go? It doesn't matter how big you have grown. You are still her baby!" Elias thought Lazar's mother must be prepared for her son's slipping into manhood. She had been through it before as Lazar was her youngest, and his two older brothers were grown braves with families of their own. She boasted her youngest son would show them he was the greatest of them all, and how Lazar might even become sachem someday.

The night before the war party's departure, there was a great bonfire, and the tribe gathered to share venison and song. Chief Pukeewis spoke to the group about the plans — who was going, with special attention to a few first-time warriors like Lazar.

"Jean-Baptiste Hertel de Rouville is leading the French militia."

Despite the purpose of the mission, Elias could not help feeling proud and happy for his friend. Drums pounded out a slow beat, and all the participants began to circle the fire in a slow dance. After what felt a long time, the beat continued with several larger drums adding a more serious tone. Lazar and the others danced as if lost in their thoughts. Elias closed his eyes and let himself enjoy the deep tones, moving gently with the beat. The ceremony continued late into the evening, but no one left. While Elias watched his friends and their families, he found himself beginning to understand what a bond they had. Their music was more moving than what he had heard in any Sunday worship.

As he let the sounds of the drums roll over him, he began to feel that things had become different, as if living with these people had changed him. He felt stronger, leaving his adolescence, stepping, like his friend Lazar, into something bigger — and exciting.

NINETEEN

FOR ELIAS, THERE had never been such a long winter. In late morning, the sun still seemed to struggle rising from behind the tall evergreens. The high trees lifted the horizon to a smaller sky that kept days short and cold. So Elias spent much of his days inside the pole lodges of his friends. They hunted and fished, but Elias enjoyed being inside by the fire more. He longed for escape and freedom and home, but now there were new thoughts too, returning often to the girl he had seen.

"Joachim," he asked, "I've heard the Jesuits have a school in the city. Have you been there?"

"No brother, I have not, but I know some who have. Why?" he laughed. "Do you want to go to school with the Black Robes?"

"No," replied Elias. "But there might be something to do there or some English speakers to talk with. Want to go there tomorrow?" The next day Joachim, and Elias, with Wematin tagging along, left the village and walked into the main part of the city to find the Jesuit school.

"That must be it," Joachim explained — "the Petit Seminary de Quebec," The building was similar to the Jesuit Seminary, made of native stone, four stories high with glass windows across each floor — maybe twenty-five each. The large, double-door entrance was heavy-looking, fastened in the middle with an iron latch. Other structures were attached in a courtyard, all with a stone base. When Elias knocked on the door, the same priest he had met at dinner months earlier invited them in.

"Hello, Father Andre," Elias said. Thank you for allowing us to be here today. We thought we would come to visit your school and speak more about France and Rome. My friends have never met a priest, and we hoped to learn about the school."

"Oh, what a pleasant surprise!" Father Andre said. "Come in, come in and make yourself comfortable. What would you like to know? I will find someone to show you around. Are you interested in learning about European culture?"

"We have a lot of time on our hands," said Elias, "I thought it might be a good way to get acquainted."

"Certainment!" said the priest. "It's good to have you here to visit. I'll send for some hot tea."

"Do you have a student here by the name of Owaissa?" Elias asked, catching the Father by surprise. "Bluebird?"

"Why yes," replied the priest, "We do. She is one of our best students. She has been here many years now — ever since she was very young. Her brothers and sisters have come too. How do you know Owaissa?"

"I saw her one day, that's all. Marguerite told me about her."

"She is not here now, but if you come back in two days, she will be. I suspect she might even like to meet you. She studies many subjects just like students in Europe. She would probably enjoy the chance to learn a bit more about English. Why don't you come back, and then I will introduce you?"

Elias was a little ashamed of his deceit in bringing his friends to the school, but it was done. And he was excited about visiting again — until they got outside, where Joachim jumped on his back, wrenching him to the ground, punishing him with punches and harsh words.

"What, Joachim?" Elias could not hide his embarrassed laugh as he covered his head to avoid the blows. Are you crazy? What?"

"Let's go to the school, Joachim! Right! You are a fool, Elias! Do you think because our skin is not like yours that we are stupid?" Elias continued an embarrassed laugh, while Joachim continued slapping. "All you wanted to do is meet Owaissa. Why didn't you just say so? You are such an English wolf!" Elias giggled and rolled over while still covering his head.

"Well, my foolish friend," continued Joachim. "I could have saved us the trip because you will not be happy when I tell you this. She is Atonwa's."

"Atonwa?" blurted Elias.

"Yes, he says it is so. When she gets a little older, maybe when the snow melts again, she will be his wife. If I were you, I'd find another maiden to stalk."

"How can that be?" asked Elias. "Did she say so?"

"She doesn't have to. Atonwa and the elders will determine."

Elias explained, "In my country, the girl decides. The men

propose, and the women say yes — they hope."

"We have something like that," said Wematin.

"Look, Joachim," said Elias, getting sterner now since this was suddenly serious business. "Has Atonwa proposed?"

"No, I don't think so. Not yet anyway. But Atonwa told us he is waiting for his chance. He is well respected and will be able to choose well — if she will have him, that is. If I were you, I'd find myself another Owaissa to dream about."

Elias was not sure what to say, but he was certain of one thing. He was not afraid of Atonwa like his friends were, and he was not about to give up this girl that easily. But now he would have to act sooner than he had thought.

TWENTY

A FEW DAYS later Elias finally met Owaissa — although they did not do much talking. She did not seem to know any English, but it did not matter since Elias found he could not find words anyway. He had never been this close to such a beauty. She sat across the room in a straight-backed chair with Father Andre, another Father and a nun, all seated in a semi-circle in the parlor. The silence was awkward, but Elias was content to sneak looks at the Indian girl while talking with the others. There was something that made her special. Her hair, or maybe it was her form, hinting from under the bright deerskin covering. While she listened to the conversation, she beamed as if smiles were just under her surface that escaped with the slightest chance.

When Owaissa looked at him, and their eyes met for the first time, Elias almost forgot where he was, struggling to hold the connection and look confident even though he felt his face flush.

"This is Elias, Owaissa," began Father Andre. "He is from the south in an English settlement. In the Boston. Isn't that right Elias?"

"Yes," Elias replied. "From Lancaster — in the Massachusetts Bay."

"Elias, Owaissa is the brightest flower in our school. She studies Latin, German and Philosophy. Someday she might like to go to Rome."

Owaissa was easily the most beautiful girl Elias had ever seen. In the room together, it was as if she made those around her fade into the background. When he finally heard her voice, an entire sentence, that is, more than just "Oui" or "No," when she spoke in several sentences, he had no idea what she had said, but the French words had poured over him like a poem. When she had finished, Owaissa smiled, and Elias knew for him, things could never be the same.

He wished he had something to give her — an excuse to touch her. He should have reached for her hand when they were introduced. For now, it would be enough to look at her and hope she would talk more so he could hear her voice again.

"Father, Andre," he asked, "Would you please ask Owaissa if she's ever met an Englishman before?" He listened to the translation and watched as the words registered with the Indian girl before a smile curled at the corners of her mouth.

Then she shook her head and said, "No."

"Me, English" Elias pointed to his chest. "From Lancaster." And that was it. He had done it. They had talked. And it was all he had hoped it could be, never imagining how a few words could be so exciting. The visit was over too soon, and he floated back to the lodge, not caring about the boys making fun of him, or how shy and embarrassed he had been or even what Joachim had said about Atonwa — how Owaissa belonged to the angry brave. The only thing that mattered now was to find someone to teach him more French — and find an excuse to go back.

TWENTY-ONE

A S THE WEATHER improved. Elias's father and John's days filled with work, their effort fueled by knowing when the mill was complete, they could go home. Construction of the mill went quickly; the foundation came together in a few weeks. John directed the placement of each log for the roof and the floor. Inside he divided the space for rooms while building the frame to hold the saw blade. There was so much to do that Elias never had a chance to return to the school as he had planned until one day he was surprised by a messenger and a note that arrived from Father Andre.

"We request for you, your father and John Bigelow, to break bread with us on Sunday next. Monsignor de Saint-Vallier and Owaissa and I enjoyed your company and would like more good conversation."

When the time came for the dinner, John felt poorly and almost stayed behind.

"You must be sick," said Thomas. "I never thought I'd see

you pass up a meal."

"You're right," said John. "I'll be fine. I'm not missing this."

The three men walked to the monastery with anticipation of another grand meal — the kind they had enjoyed when they had first arrived in Canada. Although the food turned out to be as good as expected, for Elias the dinner was long. Since he had not come for the meal, he was relieved when the priest began his speech.

"Jesuits have provided the best education the world can offer. In Europe, we have created universities to instruct deserving children of the nobility. Now we are doing the same in New France, teaching the native youth — those who show the most promise. Our students learn the wisdom of the ages: Greek, and Latin — Philosophy and Geometry. Special children like Owaissa are taught how to think just as students on the continent. Owaissa is now much like the Cleopatra who I am told learned many languages from tutors in the schools of Alexandria. With our help, the youth of this nation can do the same. Someday Owaissa will teach her children how to read and write. This is our gift to her family."

The priest talked about Owaissa in the third person — "she" this, and "Owaissa" that, like she was not sitting at the table, the same way Elias had seen other adults do when talking about their children.

"This school is only the beginning. The native children have an opportunity to learn about the true God. You know, Owaissa is a relative of the great Chief who the English called Grey Lock. Wawanotewat. He was a great warrior who fought with Metacom in your King Phillip War. Owaissa and her sister and brother are from the best stock."

When the men turned their conversation to other matters, Owaissa and Elias and the Nun, Sister Claire, eased away from the dining room. Elias was awkward as before, wondering what exactly to say, but Owaissa took the lead in breaking the nervous silence, alternating between French and Algonquin. Elias was surprised at how much he understood after spending just six months living with the natives. Brothers, sisters, father, mother, uncles — they shared freely, and he gave as well, talking about his mother and older siblings — what they did each day, how different their lives were from the Indians', about Lancaster and his life, and even what he thought his future might look like as he eased into manhood. Owaissa listened, and when it was her turn to talk, she did with surprising confidence. Elias wondered if she may have recognized many of his words from her Latin studies as they found themselves laughing and giggling while conversing easily.

Elias thought the brightness that gleamed in Owaissa's eyes revealed how happy and well-cared-for she must be. Her teeth were bright white and perfectly aligned. Her lips were full. What he would give to hold her, to feel her tenderness, to touch her face while talking gently into her ear — to kiss her mouth and smooth…

"Elias!" His father's call from the big room snapped him back. "You ready to go, Son? Time we were heading back."

On the way to their lodge, John shared what he had learned in his conversation with the priests.

"Father Jean-Pierron says the French authorities are here to establish a new world. The beaver skin trade is driving their settlement — their economy, but the Jesuits are here for religion. Their goal is to convert the Indians to Christianity —

for the Catholics and the pope in Rome."

Thomas considered what John had said and then offered his own assessment.

"I'd say it's working better than what our people tried, John. We never could find the way to get along with the Indians. Instead, we wanted everything and needed a bloodbath to get it all settled."

TWENTY-TWO

L IFE BACK IN Lancaster went on as necessary with much excitement and celebrating when the community heard the captives were alive and safe in Canada. John's wife, Jerusha, wasted little time crafting a letter to her husband, sending it with hopes he would return soon. What Jerusha could not have known was by the time her words arrived in New France, John was dying, his fever increasing each day as her letter inched its way northward.

The sickness had started as most illnesses — a headache with coughing and a general malaise. John's headache continued, and as his fever worsened, he became weaker, eventually unsteady enough to be noticed.

"You're staying here today, John. Elias and I know what to do."

"No, Thomas, I'll be alright. Moving around and working usually helps. It starts my appetite, at least."

But by the next morning, John was worse. Elias and a friend helped him to the mission with hopes more attention from the

nuns would provide John time to recover his strength. Everyone understood and accepted that a severe fever almost always
resulted in death, and Elias and his father began to fear the
worst. The nuns prepared a bed and tried concoctions and
potions to break the fever, but as John's condition worsened,
the Jesuit priests changed their focus from John's recovery to
concentrate more on saving his soul.

"Accept the faith, John," the priest coaxed. "Denounce your
Protestantism and embrace the true Catholic God. God is our
father, and he speaks through his pope on earth." John did
convert, as weak as he was, following the instructions, providing the correct responses to satisfy the Jesuits, and with what
had become no more than a dying whisper, he made promises.

"I will follow the ways of the church and encourage others
to do the same."

John would have died soon but a surprise medicine arrived
as if from God himself — Jerusha's letter. Her words spoke of
joy in hearing from her husband and her dreams of John's
return to resume the happy family life they had shared. Elias,
the nurses and Jesuit priests all listened as Thomas crouched
near the bed to read Jerusha's message directly into his friend's
ear.

"John, listen to me. Jerusha received your letter, and her
response arrived today. Listen." Thomas bent closer to deliver
Jerusha's words.

"'Dear and loving husband. In much grief and tender
affection, greatly lamenting your miserable condition,
hoping in the mercy of God who has prospered you and
kept you alive, and that He will in His own due time
work your deliverance. And I do most humbly, and

importunately petition the Governor to have pity and compassion on yourself and me.'"

Thomas must have recognized a stirring in John, so he pushed his friend more.

"John, you have to get up from this bed. You have a wife who loves you waiting at home." After Thomas had read the entire letter a fourth time, John mustered the strength to reach for the paper. He dropped his hand and paper onto his chest and closed his eyes again. Whether the letter helped, no one was certain, but to everyone's surprise and delight, John soon asked for food and began regaining strength — tiny improvement at first, before finally, as if by a miracle, he began to recover. After another two weeks, he rose, as the nuns said, like Lazarus, from what everyone had considered his deathbed — alive — and a new Catholic.

The Jesuits provide a cart for John to return to his wigwam with instructions for rehabilitation. After they had thanked the nuns and said goodbye and were on their way back, John whispered,

"Don't worry Thomas. I only agreed to make them happy. I thought it was the least I could do. I only pretended though. It was so important to them, and they were trying so hard to cure me. But I only pretended because I knew you wouldn't want to live with a Catholic!"

The two men laughed, and when they arrived at the shelter, Elias was waiting.

"We better get our bags packed, Elias."

"Right now?"

"Yes, quickly, Son. If the priests find out John tricked them, they'll build another fire for all of us."

TWENTY-THREE

WHILE JOHN RECOVERED, work continued slowly until the last day of July when the mill was nearing completion. John, Thomas and Elias sat across from Governor Vaudreuil at his dining room table eager to talk about their progress and a plan for a celebration. But the governor began their conversations with surprising news.

"You have perhaps heard, Gentlemen, about the exchange we have made with your Governor Dudley?"

"We have not," answered Thomas. "What kind of exchange?"

"Seventy-five English captives will be returning to their families in exchange for one-hundred French soldiers released from prison in Boston. One is your minister, Reverend Williams and his children — captured from Deerfield. We have negotiated for some months."

"What took so long?" John asked.

"There are many factors involved, Mr. Bigelow. You see,

our brethren are not always agreeable to release their new family members."

"You mean hostages," said John, but his comment did not elicit a response from the governor.

"That's good news Governor," said Thomas, but we want to begin making our own plans now. The mill will be complete before the new moon, and we are ready to go home. It's time to prepare."

"Yes, Thomas, I have been receiving daily reports on your progress. We are extremely pleased with what you have done. I imagine you must be very proud of your work."

"I have to admit," said John. "I had doubts. I did not expect it to come out this well. It's better than anything at home." After the governor offered congratulations, John got more to the point, pressing for their release plan. "Governor, will you be arranging our leave soon? We will need a guide."

"Yes," the governor replied. "We have to discuss your departure. You see, actually, your work here is not entirely complete."

"Not complete? Thomas's voice rose. "What do you mean? We only have a few more details to finish."

"That's right, and then you can go home, just as we agreed. But to complete the project, Thomas, we want you to teach our people how to operate the enterprise. We would like you to stay." Elias could see anger rising in his father. "We don't care which of you stays — that can be up to you. I think it should naturally fall to you, Mr. Sawyer."

John roared, slamming his hand on the table with a shout, "That was not our bargain!"

Two of the governor's bodyguards moved closer to the table

before the governor cautioned John.

"Mr. Bigelow, my assistants get nervous when people raise their voices. Please, let us not forget we are all gentlemen."

"Governor Vaudreuil." John began in a surprisingly, controlled voice. "We have been here almost a year. We have built your mill. Now we want to go home, just as we agreed."

"If you remember, Mr. Bigelow, at the time, your choices were limited. You are still our guests. Let us not forget. You can leave soon, as we have agreed, but someone will need to stay and show us how to operate the mill."

"How long?" asked Thomas.

"My people think a year should do it."

"A year!" roared John. "A year?" He jumped to his feet and almost moved toward the governor, but Thomas moved in front and extended his arms to stop him as the guards returned to the room.

"Settle down, John," Thomas said. "We'll figure this out."

"Please sit, Mr. Bigelow." The governor motioned with a delicate hand-wave to summon water. When the attendant returned with glasses for all, the tension had eased a bit, and the governor continued. "I can understand how disappointed you all must be. You've worked very hard, and I am sure you must be missing your home tremendously."

"Governor Vaudreuil," replied Thomas, "you couldn't begin to understand." Elias thought his father must have already been thinking about another year without home, and John could never stay behind.

They left the mansion, dropping down the stone steps with heavy footfalls.

"I'm sorry, Thomas, but there is just no way I can stay here another year. You know that don't you? I just cannot do it. My family needs me. I have to get back. I'm sorry. You understand, don't you?"

Thomas said he did understand, and by the time they had arrived back at their lodge, he sounded as if he had begun to resign himself to another year in Canada.

"John, you and Elias get ready to go as quickly as possible. Leave as soon as they will allow it before this French fox changes his mind. At least two of us will get back."

"Maybe you won't have to stay that long, Thomas. If they learn quickly, it might not be more than a month or two."

"Let's hope so, John. But who knows what other surprises this sly fox might have planned. If he allows you to leave, that will reveal his intentions. So get ready — plan to go right away. Trust me, John, I'll be fine."

TWENTY-FOUR

E LIAS WAS ANGRY too; it was so unfair. The reality they were still prisoners crashed around him. He hoped Governor Vaudreuil might reconsider, and since the governor was reasonable, he could be convinced to let them all go home. That was the answer; at least there was a chance.

Elias made his way to the governor's mansion, past the Jesuit mission and the school. While he walked, he practiced what he might say — what might work to sway the man's plans. He would explain how easy it was to operate the mill, and maybe the governor could understand how much they missed their families. Elias would explain that John and his father had responsibilities — they were needed at home.

By the time the large building appeared on the hilltop, Elias had formulated what he planned to say. But when he turned the corner, his thoughts were interrupted.

"Hello, Elias." He turned to see Owaissa with two other girls about her age. They were all smiling. Owaissa's friends were a bit shy-looking but sounded enthusiastic.

"I want you to meet my best friends. This is Weetow. She saw you through the window, so we rushed down the hill to see you. And this is Kaniya; we call her Swallow. They have been my classmates for a long time. We've grown up together." Elias had been surprised and had no words.

"Why are you alone?" she asked. "Where are you going?"

"I am going to see Governor Vaudreuil."

"You seem annoyed," said Owaissa. "Are you not happy we came to talk to you?"

"No, no, it's nothing like that. It's always nice to see you. And your friends are nice too. It's just now that we have the mill finished, there is a problem."

"Does it not work?" Owaissa turned and translated Elias's words to her two friends.

"The governor told us one of us, my father, needs to stay — to teach them how to operate the mill."

"Stay?" asked Owaissa. "How long?"

"He said a year, but that won't work. My father cannot stay a year. He needs to go home. We need him."

"Will you stay too?" Owaissa asked. She had been translating but now her attention remained focused on Elias.

"No," Elias said. "The governor said only one. My father agreed, but he is not happy about it. He wants us all to go. None of us can stay. John Bigelow has four young children, and he longs to return, and my father is getting along in years. He has his mill to run and the family to care for."

Owaissa translated again. Once her friends understood, Weetow whispered to Owaissa, and she passed it to Elias.

"Weetow says, what about you? Why are you not the one to stay?"

"No," said Elias, "I need to get back home too — for my father, to help at the mill. We all need to go home."

"Is someone waiting for you in your home?" Owaissa's voice was softer.

"Yes…I mean no — no one — except my mother." Elias's words felt foolish as they escaped, as he suddenly realized the meaning of Owaissa's question. "Well, I mean no one is waiting, other than my family — my mother and brothers and sisters. They probably miss me."

"Oh," said Owaissa. The three Indian girls remained quiet as Elias shifted his gaze to the governor's mansion.

"Well," Owaissa began without much conviction. "We should get back." When Elias's attention returned to the girls, he thought Owaissa looked a little sad. Until now, he had seen only sparkling happiness in her eyes, but there had passed between them strong feelings. With downcast eyes, Owaissa touched the edge of Elias's sleeve, then with Swallow and Weetow following, spun to begin the climb back up to the school.

Elias stood watching, wanting to talk more, to call to her, but the words would not come. He did not even know what he had to say. He began to walk toward the mansion and then stopped, turning to look, but the three girls had disappeared.

TWENTY-FIVE

T HE EARLY AUGUST air was hot, and swarming mosquitoes patted his face as he walked, but Elias hardly noticed as he tossed things around in his mind. He dreamed of seeing his family after being away so long — to gaze on Wachusett Mountain from the top of Prospect Hill that overlooked the Nashua River Valley — to see his older brothers and sisters again, his uncles and nieces and nephews — to give his mother the longest hug — to sit at the table enjoying a meal she would have prepared to welcome him home. He had so much to share, but now there were new feelings and none of it was enough for him to want to leave — not yet anyway.

Now he had a new plan. He turned to continue to the governor's mansion, remembering what his father had said, about the opportunity to handle the mill when he got home — all by himself. How could he have been so blind? This is perfect. Governor Vaudreuil could designate him to be the one to stay and issue an order his father had to obey.

The governor was skeptical.

"Are you sure you can handle this, Elias? It's a big responsi-bility."

Elias began in an even, confident tone. "John cannot stay, Governor. I think you understand that."

"I do, Elias. I was thirty once with a young family myself."

"My father, he's fifty-one. You have to admire his strength, but is it fair to expect him to stay another year? Especially when I am available?" Elias could see the governor was listening, so he waited for effect, then pressed on. "I am eager to do this, Governor. I will enjoy teaching everyone how to operate the mill. I am a man now, ready to make my own mark in the world without my parents standing over my shoulder."

"You make a good argument, Elias."

"But Governor, it cannot be my idea. My father will not agree unless you order it. Do you agree?"

The governor leaned back in his chair and considered Elias.

"You make a lot of sense, young man. Yes, I should make it so."

Elias left the mansion feeling satisfied his plan had worked while recalling how sad Owaissa looked when he had talked about leaving. He hoped her face would light when he sur-prised her with the news he was staying. As he trotted back to the wigwam, he remembered how she had touched his sleeve, as if with a secret message, and his excited mind raced in new ways with new possibilities.

TWENTY-SIX

"I DON'T KNOW, Elias; we need to talk about this. The governor told us he has chosen you to stay. He's ordered it. It's such a surprise. How do you feel about it?"

"It's good, Father. You go; I'll be fine."

"Are you sure?"

"I am. I want to stay." Elias could sense his father had already warmed to the idea.

"I'm not sure how I feel about it, Elias. I had resigned myself to stay. I hope you are not just saying that for my benefit. You're not worried about me, are you?"

"I don't mind staying, Father. Honest, I will learn a lot."

Mr. Sawyer continued with slow words, carefully, as if the idea were taking root.

"Well, a year would be nothing for a young buck like you. Me, on the other hand, I would not mind sleeping in my soft bed again; it sure would be nice to get back to your mother."

Elias waited, careful not to change his father's course.

"I know you've made lots of friends here, and the more I think about it, running the mill would be a great experience for you. You could learn more in one year than you could at home."

"That's right, Father."

"John's family needs him too. So that leaves you or me. And there are a lot of people depending on me. If I were a young man, I would probably feel the same. Look at it this way — this is a chance for you to do something really special. Your life in Lancaster will wait."

So it was done, and Elias recognized the yearning that grew brighter in his father's eyes with his thoughts of freedom, Hannah and home.

******

WHEN ELIAS TOLD Joachim and Lazar about their new plan, they shouted, happy and excited their English friend would be staying.

"You will stay, "yelled Lazar. "Your father goes home! Now you are truly one of us!"

Elias had a few friends in Lancaster, but they were more acquaintances, not the kind of friends he had developed here. His neighbors kept to themselves — reserved, guarded, only together one day a week, at church or to huddle in the garrison houses. The boys never hunted and fished together or talked like he did with Lazar, and Joachim and the others. Without his parents' supervision, staying in Canada would be a chance for him to finally shed adolescence and be a man. There was another not-so-small matter to consider — a good-bye to

Owaissa. Now he would not have to think about that.

As the days slid by, with only a few remaining details to complete the mill, the reality of what was happening set in — being alone. For the first time since their capture, Elias began to feel worried and uncertain — ashamed of feeling like a child without his father — not the confident man he thought he had become. Maybe he did not like the idea of being on his own as much as he had thought.

When the morning to depart arrived, the two men were up before dawn and ready to go. As Elias hugged his father with a long embrace, they did not speak, but after long moments, slapped each other on the back with man tenderness.

"Take care of yourself, Elias. I'll miss you."

Then John surprised Elias when he finished his goodbye with praise.

"We are proud of you, Elias. I am looking forward to telling your family how well you are doing — what a fine young man you've become." When John moved away, his father talked more privately, continuing their goodbyes.

"Are you sure you don't want to go back instead of me, Son? This is your last chance."

"No, I've made up my mind. I may regret it later, but I want to stay. I like these people, and I have become close to many. They have taught me a lot, father. In some ways, I feel almost part of their family."

"You certainly have learned new things, Elias — about native ways. You will be able to pass it along to our family and friends when you get home." Elias thought if he could only tell his father about Owaissa, things would be better. He was embarrassed to bring it up, but his father changed that.

"Elias, John and I wagered you must have your eye on an Indian girl. Are we right?"

Elias could not hide his surprise.

"Huh? What do you mean?"

"People talk Elias, even Indians. Fathers have a way of sniffing out this kind of thing. You forget I was young once too." Elias's father gave him a chance to react, but Elias stayed silent. "Just don't put too much stock in it and get blinded by a pretty face. Remember, Indian girls have their own people."

Elias was disappointed in his father's comment. *Own People? Were they not all just people?* What did he know about his feelings? His father had not been with Owaissa and her family in their home. Could he think because a girl was Algonquin, she was somehow less than the people in Lancaster? Why did he not understand? But Elias held his tongue so as not to ruin their farewell.

Then they were ready, and John ruffled the hair on the top of Elias's head with a reminder.

"Be careful young man. Be sure to stay away from that cranky Indian!"

Elias laughed, "Oh, don't worry about that, John."

"Come on Thomas," said John. "Get those old bones moving, and let's see if we can find our way back without getting captured again."

Elias was surprised their farewells were not sad; instead, they were oddly joyous, as if they were all turning a page to the next chapter in what was becoming an exciting adventure. The governor had been right, and now Elias felt eager for new experiences, all in a place that had become much to his liking. The farewell had not been too different than Lazar's departure a week earlier when he had left with over twenty braves, including Marguerite's uncle and Joachim's older brother. There had been the same hugs and backslaps, calling the Great Spirit to watch over each brave as they began their mission. Lazar promised Elias he would try his best not to hurt any English.

"I want to see if your English country can compare to ours, like you said, Elias, or if you have been lying to us. If I like it, I might want to move there!" Lazar promised to bring him back a present.

"Mon Amie, I'm going to capture a chicken for you — a hen that will lay you an English egg each morning!"

"Good!" laughed Elias. "But make sure you don't get a rooster by mistake!"

Elias and Lazar hugged.

"Be safe Lazar. And come back soon. We have more hunting to do."

"Keep an eye on the maidens for me," laughed Lazar. "Tell them that when I return, I will be ready to dance! As soon as Lazar returns, he's going to pick one out!"

"Sure!" yelled Elias, as Lazar moved further away." If you find one that can't run from you fast enough!" Then as Lazar and the others moved farther away, he heard his friend's big laugh from the woods.

TWENTY-SEVEN

W HEN ELIAS APPEARED at Owaissa's wigwam, she was away visiting a friend, but her mother sent for her, and it was not long before Owaissa returned.

"Elias. I did not expect to see you here. The messenger said you wanted to see me. Is everything all right?"

"Well, yes." Elias started, still struggling with what he wanted to say and how he was going to say it. "You know the mill is almost complete, right?"

"Yes, you said before. You must be pleased, no?"

"Yes, well no," Elias stammered.

"Are you leaving soon — come to say goodbye?"

"No," said Elias."

"Then what is the matter? I do not quite recognize you. Why do you have such a heavy heart today? Is your father and John Bigelow not well? Did they not return to your Lancaster?"

"Yes, they left this morning."

Owaissa studied Elias's face and waited as if to understand

his mood, but he only squatted inside the lodge, scratching the dirt, his gaze locked on a stick.

"It's not that. I'm not sad, Owaissa. I'm happy. Nervous, that's all."

They remained silent in the heavy quiet, packed with what Elias had come to say. When he finally looked up from his dirt lines, Owaissa was smiling.

"Now that your mill is complete, you do not want to leave — to say goodbye? Is that it?" Elias was caught off guard by her awareness and struggled for his next words. Owaissa continued before he could speak. "I understand. It is difficult to leave people you have come to know." Elias waited for more. "And those people… who you might even love…who you care about…" Elias smiled, sensing Owaissa was the one floundering now.

"Look, Owaissa. I know you know this. I want to stay here. I want to spend more time with you, from the first day. There, I said it. You like talking with me. Isn't that right?" Owaissa let Elias continue, waiting for him to look up from the ground again. But he did not, speaking without lifting his head to face her with his full attention remaining on his stick.

"It's just that I was hoping to get to know you better, that's all." He started to say more, but instead as if tangled in his words, he stood up and flipped the stick into the fire. "I must go now. Then, without another look, he stepped out the flap of the wigwam.

TWENTY-EIGHT

WORK AT THE mill absorbed all of Elias's time and concentration. He liked feeling a more important part of the project and the attention he was receiving as an expert in the mill enterprise. After so much time spent working alongside his father in their Lancaster mill, Elias knew the workings of the mill. Now it was so important to perform well as everyone was watching, interested in the mill's structure and mechanics. During construction, carpenters had come often to study the new mill's components while recording calculations and engaging Elias's father and John in discussions for the next mills they were planning. Now Governor Vaudreuil began to send lieutenants and planners regularly with more detailed questions for Elias.

Father Andre was a regular visitor as well. For one visit, the priest brought an unusually large group of students including Owaissa and two young French soldiers.

"Elias, since we have emphasized the significance of the

new mill for New France, we felt a field trip was in order. These young men who have joined us today are part of the Army of France — Les Troupes de la Marine. Let me introduce, Jen Veld dit Sansoucy, and Pierre de St. Ours." Elias greeted the men who looked younger than he thought a soldier would be — not much older than himself. "Almost three years ago, they traveled from France to protect our country from the Iroquois who raid from the west and also the English in the Ohio." Father Andre spoke in French, interspersed with some English words, stopping often to explain to Elias. After eighteen months, Elias had begun to understand French well enough and did not need much of the translation.

"When their tour of duty is completed, they plan to stay. For men their age, like you, Elias, there is more opportunity here than back in France." Elias was curious.

"Father Andre, ask them if they are looking forward to ending their soldier's life."

After the priest's translation, Pierre answered with French and Abenaki,

"Oui monsieur, very much! And you, are you returning to your home, or will you stay in Canada like us?"

"I will be leaving when the training is done," Elias replied.

Father Andre continued,

"As an incentive to remain and settle, the soldiers will each receive a 'concession' from the French government of a sizable portion of land. They will marry and start families."

As Elias listened, his mind wandered. His eyes followed Owaissa as she moved and talked with the students who had crowded into the mill. Seeing her in these different surroundings made an impression. *Could she possibly be more beautiful than the last time he had seen her weeks ago?* He wanted to be near her, to hear her voice, even if much of the time he did not know what she was saying. It was enough to watch her move, to hear her include his name jumbled with her French and Abenaki sentences. What he did not like was her talking and laughing with the two soldiers — especially Pierre who stood always close to her.

"Elias," began Father Andre, "why don't you show us how things work?" Elias explained how the mill had been designed — how the water moved the outside wheel to turn the saw blade inside. But as he talked, it was difficult to concentrate. He wanted them to leave because he had to sort things out fast. Now it was not just Atonwa he was worried about. It was Pierre and others like him who were lurking with big "concessions" and plans for families. After the group left, he decided it didn't matter that he was English and she Algonquin. He would need to act fast and not let this beauty get away.

TWENTY-NINE

WHEN ELIAS FINALLY got his chance to see Marguerite, she was willing to help.

"I will talk to her father," she said. "I will tell him you would like to visit the family. He will agree if I ask. After that, my little brave, the rest will be up to you. It can be said you will need to paddle that canoe yourself." While they both laughed, Elias jumped and planted a kiss on Marguerite's cheek.

One afternoon a few days later, an Indian boy delivered an invitation.

"Owaissa's father would like you to join his family for a special meal — at tomorrow's sunset. Come to their lodge. You will accompany the family of Owaissa to the longhouse of Pukeewis. He is the chief of our tribe." The messenger waited for a response that was a long time coming because Elias could not find the words.

The chief's lodge was longer than the other wigwams, with enough room for several families. The longhouse was dark inside, except light from the large fire blazing in the middle with smoke rising through the open flap in the roof. Since it was hot inside, the entrance flap along with another side flap was left open to let in air.

When they had settled, the chief's wife, Marie, offered earthen plates filled with hot squash and pumpkin, then passed a large bowl of corn. She eased corn cobs still wrapped in the husks, from coals near the edges of the fire. Outside, a small deer turned on a spit. Marie cut pieces while scurrying in and out of the longhouse, keeping everyone supplied with meat.

Elias thought Chief Pukeewis looked like a happy man, surrounded by an excited family who included seven children: four boys and three girls, all under fifteen. His wife was Marie Tekanonnens, his second; his first, he explained, died of measles. The children drifted among the adults, encouraging attention while playing with their toys. Each girl had a corn cob doll adorned exactly like a native woman. They wore nothing more than breechcloths. The two small girls took turns snuggling with their father. While Owaissa combed one of the young girl's hair, she introduced the children.

"This is Marguerite; she's five. And this," she added as the older girl squirmed against her side, "is Tannhahorens. She is seven. They're my nieces, and I love them like sisters!"

Elias watched Owaissa play with the girls and laughed when they jumped on her and knocked her over. When he crunched a twig under his nose to amuse the little ones, they crowded closer, sometimes mimicking his strange words.

"Me, Elias! Who you?" The new language did not matter to the little ones as they were soon snuggled, one girl under each of Elias's arms, holding their dolls while listening to the adults talk. He enjoyed their time together. Pukeewis was interested in what Elias had to say and wanted to know why the English hated native peoples. He knew much about the settlers' treatment of the Pequot and the Wampanoags' war.

"English worse than Iroquois. English wants us go. Soldiers drive Wampanoag from our home. They drive French from Quebec. French are friends. Maybe we can be friends with English — like you. Are others like Elias in your land?"

"I'm not that different from the others. We just want to live in peace too." Elias found difficulty defending some of what the chief described, but they agreed if the English and the Indians could learn to respect each other, things would be better for the children.

Pukeewis used flint to spark a smoke in his calmut, a stone pipe with a long tube adorned with feathers of various sizes and colors. When he had the fire burning correctly he passed the pipe, and they all shared the tobacco, the first for Elias. As the pipe moved and the tobacco smoke filled the wigwam with a pleasant smell, the mood was changing as they relaxed. Elias tried to keep Owaissa in his sights, catching her eyes and looking from her to her mother, to her father and the chief. Even across the cultures, it was as if they all could see what was happening.

When he and Owaissa's family strolled back to her lodge, Elias moved as close as he dared. With more to say, words came more easily as they talked about her schooling, and he was eager to share information about Lancaster. Owaissa asked about the girls — what did they wear, and what did they do each day. Did they work like Indian women, and when did they marry? And about him — what did he do in Lancaster? Elias

found he liked talking about things he had never before —
family dynamics — who talked and spent time with whom —
how the minister was the leader of the community, and how
important a man he was.

"He's like a chief — specially trained in God's word. He
teaches people the right way to live. Each settlement has a
minister."

"You don't have priests like the Jesuits?"

"No, no priests. That's Catholic. We're Protestants."

"I do not understand about your different religions. There
are too many."

"I'm not sure about all of it either. We don't have a pope —
that's one thing. Other than that, I don't know. British are
Protestants and French are Catholic...that's the way it has
been. Same God though."

"Our people don't have different religions. You white men
are confused. I've learned you have killed each other about
God?"

"You're right; it is foolish!" They walked a bit more, and
Elias felt more alive next to the Indian girl, even comfortable
with the occasional periods of quiet. It felt natural they did not
have to talk all the time, enough just being together.

"So, what do you believe, Owaissa — about God?"

"God is in everything," Owaissa spoke confidently. "He is
the Great Spirit in all things. You've heard of this?"

"Sure."

"The trees and plants and animals, the rivers, even the
rocks and the mountains — they all have spirit — the same as
the people. We are all one."

"Elias responded, "It's not that simple."

"No? Why do you need churches and ministers and priests and popes to tell you what to think? The Indian listens to his heart. Our God is within."

"It's in the Bible," said Elias. "We follow what it says in the Bible. God's book."

"God wrote in a book?"

Elias laughed. "No, men did — but they're God's words — the way to live."

"The People don't need a book. Our elders teach us how to live. Grandfathers teach the boys — grandmothers the girls. Since the beginning that has always been the way."

"Well, in Lancaster, we have Reverend Prentice to teach us. He is the fourth minister — from the beginning of the town."

"And the others?"

"The first one left when the Indians burned all the houses. The second one was killed in a raid, and the third one, Reverend Gardiner, he died last year — shot by the sentinel."

"The guard? Why did the guard shoot him?"

"He thought he was an Indian sneaking into the house." When Owaissa looked confused, they both began to laugh, and she asked again about the English God.

"Is your God a good God — or is he wrathful?" The question surprised Elias, deeper than he would have expected — more like a question a minister would ask and surely the effect of Owaissa's education.

"I think he's a little of both. He punishes and rewards, depending on how you behave."

They grew quiet and with the walk over, Elias said goodbye to everyone before extending his hand for Owaissa — the only contact he dared. Her hand was soft and alive — warm, exciting. A spark of desire pulsed through his arm and into his mind. If they had been alone, he would have dared to snatch her to his chest. For now, he could only let himself absorb her gaze, releasing her hand only when he felt he must.

"Good night," he said, first to Owaissa's mother and then to her father. "Thank you for this blessing. This has been a wonderful visit, and I look forward to seeing you all again very soon."

On the way back, Elias found himself thinking new, exciting thoughts — how his life could be. He would return to Lancaster with an Indian beauty to show off and be the envy of his older brothers and his friends with the angel he had discovered in the north woods. How his parents would love and adore her. He would build her the best house near them — cut and saw the boards himself and ask John Bigelow to help. They would have many children who would play at his feet like Pukeewis enjoyed and /sit with him in the meetinghouse pew each Sunday like other families. Owaissa would teach them Indian ways, and their children would live as English. She would love him, and he would be happy...just like Pukeewis.

THIRTY

"ELIAS, GET UP, you lazy toad!" Awasos yelled from outside the lodge. He was with Joachim, Rowi and Wematin. They had come for Elias, waking him at dawn to deliver their exciting news. Elias climbed from under his bearskin and pushed the flap back from the wigwam opening to greet them.

"What are you doing here so early?"

"We came for you." Joachim gushed. "We have great news to share!"

"So, come inside then; it's too cold out there. Come in where it's warm. We can talk here."

Elias offered skins to each, and when the four visitors were comfortable, Awasos burst the news.

"Atonwa, he chose us for the next raid!"

"We are all going," Joachim added. "Our first one!" Elias considered the news but had nothing to say. He was surprised and confused.

"When is the raid?" he asked. "Where are you going?"

"We don't know," said Joachim. "Atonwa knows where, but he won't say. It will be soon though."

"Can you believe it? The four of us — on a real raid!" Awasos looked more excited than Elias had ever seen him.

"Don't you wish you could…?" Wematin's sentence hung unfinished. "I'm sorry, Elias, I'm not thinking. That would not be good for you, would it?"

"Not really, you moose. What am I going to do, raid my own village?"

They looked at each other for long moments, as if expecting each other to talk before Joachim got back to what had excited them.

"Matun told Atonwa for our first raid we will stay in the rear to protect the others. That is what everyone does the first time. As soon as the raid is over, and our men are fleeing, we stay behind to slow anyone that might be pursuing."

"The rear guard?" said Elias.

"Yes," said Joachim. "The rear guard. Matun said it is an important job — the way to earn respect. We distinguish ourselves by protecting the others."

"Well, I wish you luck, but I'm not going to be around to see how it comes out."

"Why not?" asked Joachim.

"Because I have plans — big plans of my own. As soon as the training is complete, I am leaving here." Then Elias paused to look at each of his friends before finishing. "I am going home!"

"When?" asked Joachim. "Why?"

"Soon, I hope. As soon as the governor agrees. Just have to say my goodbyes, and then I'm on my way."

"Come on brother — we have a lot of hunting to do. And I thought a certain someone might have something to say about it. Are you sure you want to go?"

"Oh, yes, well, that's part of the plan — the good news that is. I might take Owaissa with me."

"What?" blurted Joachim. "To white man's country?"

"No!" shouted Wematin. "You cannot take Owaissa back with you."

"Oh no? We'll see about it."

"What about Atonwa?" asked Joachim.

"What about him?"

"Atonwa would never allow that. He plans to marry Owaissa."

Elias looked at each of the boys as they waited for his reaction. Then he offered with few words what must have appeared to his friends as a very brave answer. After he had pulled his deerskin robe tight, Elias left the boys watching his back as he spoke over his shoulder, "Just know this, my friends. Your leader Atonwa, he is not part of my plans." Then he ended his response and stepped out into the cold morning to relieve himself.

THIRTY-ONE

SEVERAL MEN FROM the government office spent the morning at the mill. When they had finally left, Elias was alone and had a surprise. Two female visitors, one almost Owaissa's age and another about nine, slipped up near the mill door and spoke through the open top half.

"English?" The younger girl whispered.

"Hello there," answered Elias. "Who are you?" The girls wore traditional deerskin coverings with beads attached to their armbands and the bottom hems of their top covering. The older girl's hair was black, hanging in tight braids down her back. The younger girl's skin was white; her red hair was braided the same. In a quiet voice, the white girl introduced them.

"This is my friend, Gabrielle. She is Red Flower. She wants me to talk English for her. I am Martha Fairbanks."

"You are English then?"

"I was," said Martha. "I am Missoui now."

"You came to see the mill?" Elias thought that unlikely.

"Red Flower says she comes to talk. Her brother is Atonwa." Red Flower began to speak to Martha in Wabanaki with part French, enough for Elias to understand much without Martha's translation. Although the girls seemed genuine, Elias was wary, and when he followed his instinct to glance outside to see if others might be lurking, Martha responded,

"We came alone," she said.

"Does Atonwa know you are here?"

"No," Martha replied while passing the question to Red Flower and waiting for directions. Red flower spoke in Wabanaki, and Martha translated. "If my brother knew we had come, I don't know what would happen. He would be angry with both of us. I am afraid what he might do."

"Yes, I've noticed your brother can be excitable!" Elias thought humor could be good medicine. "So, Martha, ask Red Flower what I can do for her?" Since she was related to Atonwa, Elias was anxious to have the girl say what she wanted and be on her way.

"Please leave," Red Flower said. "As soon as you can."

Elias could not stop his laugh.

"You laugh," Red Flower remarked through Martha. "You don't know what my brother might do."

"Oh, but you're wrong about that, Red Flower. I do have an idea what Atonwa might do!" Elias let his remark sink in before continuing. "But there is a lot to consider."

"Yes, I know," said Red Flower. "We know. It is Owaissa. We all know."

Elias had continued sharpening the saw, but now the girls had his full attention.

"How do you know these things?"

"Owaissa is my friend since we have been children. When we are together, she teaches me letters and reads to me from her books and the catechism for Catholics — and words from other languages she has learned. We talk about everything." Red Flower watched Elias absorb her words and glanced again toward the trail leading to the woods. Elias saw another Indian girl hiding and watching on the edge of the woods. Then Martha passed more words.

"We say no stay — leave. Take Owaissa with you if you must, English — to your lands. But soon. Go to your own country. Red Flower, she say you should hurry!"

"That's not a bad idea, but I'm not sure it's the best one." Elias realized he had to stop his superior demeanor. Atonwa's sister had surely risked her safety to come to help him — or more accurately, to warn him.

"I'm sorry Red Flower, I appreciate you coming here, but the French have made me stay until the training is done."

"Don't care what French want," Red Flower insisted. "We help you leave. I will guide you until you are safe. You could be far away before anyone learns. We tell Owaissa, and you leave soon while the moon is bright. The way will be clear enough to travel." Elias was amazed at what he was hearing.

"That would be dangerous for you — and me. Why would you do that?" Red Flower was quiet. As she sat, she looked at her hands that she held folded in her lap. Elias waited for long moments before the girl spoke, this time without looking up from her hands.

"It is Atonwa," she began, "Je vous assassinerai....... a la morte!"

"He will kill you," explained Martha. "Red Flower heard them planning." Elias tensed, as never before.

"When?" he blurted. "I mean how?" His mind was racing. "Who with?"

"When they return from their big raid. If you are here when he returns, he says he comes for you — with his friends."

"When will that be?"

"I am not sure, but it has been a moon since they left. They plan to rendezvous with many others in the south." Red Flower waited for Elias to respond, but when he remained silent, she gave Martha more words. "The French have arranged a new raid. Other tribes are joining — many braves. Atonwa boasted to his friend's sister who told me. He has been chosen as a leader for the first time. Many of his friends and younger braves are going as well. Hawk and Rowi — even White Tail. Some of your friends too. You have time, but you should not wait. They could be back soon."

And that was it. The warning had been delivered. Elias thanked the girls before they slipped out as quietly as they had come, trotting toward the trailhead where two other girls stepped out of the opening before all disappeared as if the trees had swallowed them.

Elias was frightened thinking about Atonwa and what he might do. For the first time in his life, he felt fear that could only come from being alone.

THIRTY-TWO

Elias was near his wigwam when a strange scream of women's voices erupted, jerking him out of his thoughts. A raiding party slid into the camp, but without excitement and what the People called, a "grand bal." The faces of the men betrayed bad news. Near the back of the group, where the line stretched out behind, two braves carried a body lying over two poles until they reached the lodge of Magmos where they lowered the body to the ground. With frantic screams from the women, it was difficult to hear. He did not want to see, but with a pounding heart, Elias forced himself to look and realized the worst. The dead brave was Lazar.

Some tried to calm Lazar's mother, but she could not be consoled as she wailed and threw herself across her son's body. Elias noticed a crimson splotch on Lazar's side, and the hair on the side of his friend's head was matted in dried blood. When he moved to kneel beside his friend's body, Elias reached to touch Lazar's shoulder with just the tips of his fingers, then pulled his hand back.

"Lazar, you stupid," he whispered as if the brave would hear. "I told you. Why weren't you careful? What did you have to go for — to die?" His friend's spirit was gone — the body cold and stiff. Elias brushed away tears before looking up to see the pain in the eyes of everyone around him. One by one, the men and women crouched to touch Lazar's body in respect. When Elias noticed some of the men crying, his quiet tears turned to angry sobs, and he was not ashamed. The big brave, Roussin, came close and grabbed Elias, circling his arms in a rough hug, his shoulders heaving with heavy sobbing too.

"He was like my little brother, Elias!" Roussin released Elias and pulled Lazar's body close, lifting him like a doll. His cries caused the others to cry harder. Fathers, mothers, and friends — they all milled around Lazar's body. Even the children came near with no apparent direction from their parents, curious about death but respectful of the fallen brave. Some touched the body, but most just stood close. Then Elias was surprised by a familiar voice.

"Elias." The voice was startling because it was English and a young one at that. He turned to see a boy, not more than seven or eight years old, standing near the flap of the wigwam. He had a proud air with a firm stance. His feet were shod with moccasins with his chest and shoulders covered with a deerskin smock. His leggings were deerskin as well, and he carried a knife on a belt that cinched his waist.

"Don't you remember me, Elias?"

Elias searched for a name. "Simon!" he finally shouted with a slap at his thighs. Look at you! I didn't even recognize you!" Elias took more time to look the boy over. "Look, your hair, it's so long!"

The boy lifted one leg to show his moccasins. Elias was curious about a smaller boy, dressed the same, who stood beside Simon.

"Who is your friend, Simon?"

"He's Joshua. He's six; he's been here longer than me."

"Where are you from, Joshua?"

"He won't talk to you. He's from Deerfield. He told me they took many — killed his parents too. He saw them do it."

Elias had heard of many other captives from Massachusetts Bay and the killing during the Deerfield attack, so he thought it best to change the subject.

"Your relatives won't recognize you when you return, Simon. They're probably worried sick about you."

"I don't think so. I live with Assacambuit now anyway — in his family. I have two sisters too: Angeni and Gabrielle." Elias was unsure how to respond as Simon continued. "I like it here. I like them, and they like me. They are good to me."

"You don't want to go home, Simon?"

"I'm not sure; I mean no. I don't want to walk that long way. And I want to stay here so Assacambuit can teach me to hunt. He even said so."

"That's not a decision you need to make yet. You still have a lot of growing to do, Simon. Give it some time. When I am ready to return, you can come with me — your sister too."

"Molly? She will not come either. I see her sometimes, and she looks like all the others. You would not even know her. She told me she was adopted by Tamyasisa. Molly likes it here too. She told me!"

Simon and Joshua were two of the many children who stood and stared at Lazar's body while Elias wondered what the boys might be thinking. He moved close to Simon, placing his hand on his shoulder, but the boy jerked away as if there was a distance between them.

"What happened?" Simon asked. "Lazar died?"

"Yes, Simon, he's dead."

"Who killed him?"

"I don't know…the English."

"Why? Did he do something bad?"

Elias struggled to explain things to Simon — about the raid.

"I don't know." Elias lied. "They fought, I guess. They must have been afraid Lazar would hurt them."

"Lazar was my friend," Simon said, and then he was quiet. Elias scanned the faces surrounding Lazar's body, and when he looked back for Simon, the boy was gone. The wails of the women continued into the evening when Elias finally got the story from Sawatis.

"We traveled seven days," past Champlain — west, then south to the Connecticut River. We stumbled on English militia soldiers who were just as surprised. There were many, so we ran, but Lazar got shot in the side." Sawatis was fighting tears and stopped talking to compose himself.

"He was so brave, Elias! He turned to fight more, but the English bullet stung him behind his ear. We carried him two days, but off and on he lost consciousness and finally died — two nights ago. My heart is sad; I cannot tell you."

Elias did not have to hear about Sawatis's sadness. He had grief of his own. When Matun appeared at the funeral, people clustered around the warrior-hero, surprised at his show of sadness. Matun was still an imposing presence to Elias causing both admiration and fear. When he saw Elias, the big man came closer.

"English! Comment allez-ous?"

"Hello, Matun. I'm sorry about your loss."

"Sorry?"

"Yes, Lazar was my friend."

"Friend? English?" Matun's voice was more a grunt. "The People, they are not your friends! You kill; we kill." They stared at each other, and then the war chief turned as if surveying the group before stalking away, walking slowly with not another word.

After much chanting and crying, the people finally gathered to bury Lazar's body. While the women continued to wail, the braves carried themselves with stern resignation, as if accepting death. Many commented that Lazar would have been a great man. Elias thought hard about how sad he was and what Matun had said about killing. *English and Indian — so alike. Why did we have to kill each other?*

During the funeral gathering, the drums beat a steady thump. When Elias spotted Owaissa standing with her friends, his emotions jumbled with punishing grief for Lazar mixed with excitement as he approached the three Indian girls. He greeted Owaissa's friends with polite courtesy before swallowing Owaissa in a quiet, spontaneous embrace. He held her close for several moments before he took her hand, leading her away from her friends and the crowd.

They walked out of sight just inside the edge of the woods. It was dark, and he did not try to stop himself before he turned and kissed Owaissa for the first time. She lifted her arms, sliding her hands and arms along his shoulders, clutching him as his kiss continued. Her fingers pressed, encouraging him before a tiny sound escaped through her throat. When their kiss ended, he held his cheek against hers and then kissed her again, harder this time, his hands moving first across her back, then under her arms, sliding his hands along her sides to the rise of her hips. When Owaissa's hands found the back of his head, her lips insisted, pressing hard against his. As he pulled her close, his mind raced when Owaissa lifted her mouth to his ear and whispered,

"I like it to be kissing you, my English boy."

They eased their way back to the group, with Elias no longer caring who might notice them walking together or what others would think — even Atonwa.

THIRTY-THREE

TIME DRAGGED WHILE Elias counted the days before he could go home. After a dark, cold winter waiting for the thaw, his work routine at the new mill consumed the new spring and summer with teaching workers the skill and nuances of log cutting. Now, in early August, days were still warm, but evenings had become cooler and nights were cold. The People had been enjoying fresh corn for weeks; the squash and large, orange pumpkins were ripe. A few trees in lower, marshy areas showed a slight color tint, the leaves announcing an end and a beginning, reminding Elias of home.

One afternoon, after an unexpected message arrived, the workers in the mill laughed watching Elias skip, lifting his knees and clapping his hands on his thighs, his moccasins quietly patting the smooth oak floor. He jumped and hollered in silly celebration until he'd tired. Then while waving a note from the governor like a flag, he addressed the curious onlookers,

"I'm going home!"

There would still be a few more weeks of work until he was free. One late afternoon, as the sun was almost lost behind the high evergreens on the top of the western hill, Elias closed the mill door and fastened the iron latch. A heavy-looking bank of clouds edged to swallow what was left of the sun, making the evening dark earlier. With thoughts of dinner, his steps quickened moving away from the mill to begin the three-mile walk back to the village. A lightening spark lit the dark sky behind the tree line and was followed, after a breath, by the angry rumble of thunder rolling from behind the hills.

Several hurried strides from the mill door, Elias stopped short, startled by a dark form approximately the distance of two or three longhouses away, standing directly in his path. The body was that of a man, its shape a silhouette with shoulders, neck and head melting together. As the form moved toward Elias, a man's features became clearer. It had been over a year, but there could be no mistaking — it was Atonwa. He had blackened under his eyes and still looked defiant but a little different — bigger than Elias remembered — bare-chested, dressed only with breechcloth, staring with the same menacing look. He was more mature-looking, taller than Elias recalled and wider with thicker arms and legs.

Elias's friends had shared that from an early age, Atonwa had been a battler with French youths as well as others from inside and outside the tribe. His grandfather was a renowned fighter, and Atonwa had been watched, gaining the respect of elders and peers early — recognized as a good man to have on your side.

In one hand, Atonwa held a dark-colored, French iron ax

that hung with the head almost touching the ground. The white bone handle of the eight-inch knife Atonwa had brandished in their fight still topped the scabbard on his belt. Elias noticed at least two of Atonwa's friends who had remained yards back, almost hidden near the edge of the woods.

Since Atonwa must have been waiting for the workers to leave, Elias had no doubt this visit could only mean trouble. He stood waiting for the brave to speak, and when Atonwa began, it was just a growl.

"You still here, English. When you go?"

Because of the distance, Atonwa's voice was a shout.

"Where?" Elias replied, keeping his voice loud.

"You know — to your land."

Elias was wary. "Not sure. Soon, I hope, but I need to talk with the French. It's up to them."

"No want you here." Atonwa swept his free arm in an arc as he spoke. "This ours. You go before I am coming back." Elias began to understand the full purpose of the visit and glanced again toward the trees where Atonwa's friends remained.

"Why do you hate me, Atonwa?"

"You are English; English is snake."

Elias responded while attempting to use logic as a salve, mixing Abenaki, French and English.

"Look, Atonwa, I didn't ask to come here. Remember? I have tried to get along with everyone and…"

"Stop words," Atonwa barked. While Atonwa's hate and anger bubbled, Elias stiffened. "Talk too much — you no talk my people!" Elias knew what Atonwa meant but he didn't want to get dragged into that.

"Look, I can't help what's happened — how I feel. Some

things you just do not control. I'm sorry about that, Atonwa, I really…" but Atonwa cut him off.

"Hear me, English! No more talk!" With a loud, scream, the warrior spun on his heels in a circle, swinging the iron hatchet with his arms extended before, with a loud grunt, releasing the weapon in Elias's direction. Elias lunged to the side as the ax whizzed by, its form tumbling over itself, cutting the air with a trailing hiss before crashing into the wooden door, the wide blade embedding deep into the wood with a dull thud. As if in triumph, Atonwa let out another war cry as he and Elias stared at the ax.

Atonwa's demeanor changed with the approaching weather and deepening darkness. He sauntered near enough to almost touch Elias, passing on to the mill where after much effort with forceful tugs, he pried the ax from the wood. Now, with a potentially deadly attacker between him and the door, Elias fought panic — afraid, angry at himself for being so careless, the same way he had been at the mill when he and his father were captured. Elias stared at Atonwa and waited, feeling like a target — no match for an attacker with a deadly weapon. *Should I run? If only I had my musket!*

Elias stood paralyzed in the same spot, ready for what could happen next. As he watched Atonwa, he wondered what his chances might be to get inside for the wood ax — especially considering Atonwa's friends were still close. Atonwa had quieted, but Elias was not fooled. His muscles tensed with a feeling of power and excitement only danger could create. If he ran, Atonwa's ax might find his back, or his braves would track him down before he could reach the village. Elias fought to disguise his fear and plan. It was all he could do to stand still, measuring the distance to charge Atonwa. If the brave whirled again to throw the hatchet, Elias would duck and rush to get to Atonwa's legs.

When the remaining sun disappeared behind the black bank of rain clouds, Atonwa looked up, then toward the woods as if the tension had broken. He began to walk, and when he strode past Elias, he stopped to lean in near with his face close to Elias's, in a soft, threatening voice, he practically spit in slow, taunting words.

"You go, English — before I am coming back." Then, in no apparent rush, he continued, walking the distance to his friends.

When they all disappeared into the woods, Elias wasted no time, scurrying back inside the mill to retrieve his wood ax. As a stiff wind blew the first curtain of cold rain, he hurried north along the path to the village, glancing back repeatedly — afraid of whom he might encounter. Under the trees, absent the remaining twilight, it was almost dark. He had to be careful — examining the trail ahead, listening before every turn, as he picked his way along the path, the cold rain almost insignificant. In drenching storms during their long march from Lancaster, he had learned how to ignore physical conditions. His thoughts now, like before, were re-focused on just staying alive. From now on, he would avoid being alone — and never without his ax.

He was still a servant, so he would expect no help; he would have to leave before Atonwa returned. But it would not change things about Owaissa. He decided he would take her with him. And that would solve everything.

THIRTY-FOUR

ELIAS MADE THE visit he had been dreaming about; he would make Owaissa his. Although he had arrived confident, now he began to feel uncertain, small while setting low in the chair in front of the Monsignor de Saint-Vallier's enormous desk.

"Father, I would like you to marry Owaissa and me as soon as possible. I want to take her back to Lancaster." Elias waited for the answer he expected, but the priest was quiet until he finally leaned forward on his elbows as if to emphasize important words to come. After a pause, the priest spoke deliberately, delivering words carefully in a practiced-sounding tone, almost as if to lecture.

"My Son, that is not possible." The priest showed none of his usual cordiality. "Owaissa is of high breeding with favored station among her people. She is one of our New France aristocrats, her uncle a chief who has no surviving sons. Owaissa will choose wisely for marriage, and someday she could even be sachem." The priest waited as if in a practiced fashion to allow his words to settle. "Elias, you must understand — Owaissa is Catholic. You are Protestant. The two do not mix. And we do not approve."

Mix. Approve? As the priest continued, Elias's head was spinning as if he had been hit.

"No. It would be a sin for Owaissa to marry outside the church and become a Protestant. She would lose the state of grace. And since your children would not know the true God, they would be denied heaven." Elias tried to absorb what he had heard, holding back, waiting even when the priest paused again as if to allow a reply or to prepare more information. Then Elias struggled for the best logic with which to respond.

"It's different with me and Owaissa."

"I'm sorry, my Son. The pope is strict with these matters. You would need to be a Catholic — to convert, but that could never happen in your colony."

"Why not?"

"You are not aware of your English law? They do not allow Catholics."

"I don't care about any of that. I love her, and she loves me. She said so."

"Well, Elias, you need to care about it. These are important matters. The worst thing you could do is take Owaissa from her home and deny her and her future children a life with God. That would be selfish of you."

Elias sat stunned. The Monsignor studied him to measure the effect of his words until Elias stood to leave, sliding his steps as if in a daze. While they walked through the hall to the door, the priest finished his admonition.

"It's difficult, I know, Elias — these things we humans do. But we need to trust in God; he will lead us on the path to happiness. You must think of Owaissa as well — her future — what's best for her. Return to your people, Elias. Leave Owaissa with hers. Allow her to be happy. It's best for everyone."

Elias's steps were slow and heavy as he made his way toward his wigwam, the Jesuit's words squeezing his heart. He passed people in the village, but if they had tried to acknowledge him with eye contact, he would not have noticed, lost as he was in his thoughts. He had just never thought about such important things before. *Could he let the French God stop him from marrying Owaissa? Could their God be this cruel?*

THIRTY-FIVE

M ARGUERITE'S FACE LOOKED warm and content to Elias as she scrapped kernels from ears of corn into a stone bowl. Her long brown hair was braided in two strands that bounced with her movements, tapping her forearms while she worked. Although her girls, Malgelit and Malian, scurried through the area, climbing in and out of the longhouse, Marguerite remained absorbed with her task until she stopped and leaned away from the bowl when she had finally recognized Elias's lingering gaze.

"What do you want to tell me, my English man? Or are you going to just sit there until I drag it from you?"

"You noticed? You are wiser than I thought."

"Wise enough."

"Will you not tell anyone?" Marguerite was quiet while she considered Elias.

"This has got to be about a girl, doesn't it?"

"Come on, Marguerite. Do you want me to talk about it or not?"

"I think if you don't, you are going to burst." Elias did not look up.

"It's Owaissa. I love her."

"Oh, love." Marguerite acted more interested now but turned her attention back to the bowl and her grinding.

"Love? That's nice. Does Owaissa know this?"

"Yes, she loves me too."

"Now that is interesting. And when did this all happen?"

"It's been happening for a while — months — ever since the first time I saw her."

Marguerite stopped working again, this time moving to sit beside Elias as if the conversation had become more serious.

"I must be older than I thought. I never saw this coming. Who else knows about you two?"

"I don't know, some of my friends must suspect. Joachim for sure — maybe everybody by now. I think her mother sees." When Elias had finished with the names, he added, "and Atonwa."

Marguerite pushed on her knees and rose to return to her work, deliberately, as if making time to fully consider what Elias had said. Elias waited for her to respond while he busied himself, making sparks rise in the smoke of the campfire with a stick he pushed at the burning logs.

"Atonwa, Elias? Did you know he has said he would marry Owaissa? Have you heard that?"

"I know, I know," Elias groaned. "My friends told me. But I don't care."

"Well, as far as Atonwa is concerned, I never liked the idea of that match. But it is up to Owaissa. Atonwa cannot have whoever he wants. We'll just have to see what she wants." Elias tossed a stick with a yellow flame onto the fire before finally saying what he had come to ask.

"So Marguerite, what do you think — I mean about Owaissa and me?"

Marguerite smiled and turned back to her scraping. "I've seen worse matches."

"Seriously, I want to take her home with me — to Lancaster." Marguerite continued to work, but after more silent moments, came close to Elias again and sat, placing her hand on his knee.

"Elias, do you think she could be happy in your land?"

"Of course! I'll build her a house — a strong one, near my parents, and we'll have a good life."

"It's not you who would be the problem. It's others — wives and mothers especially. They would not accept her as one of their own. She would find herself isolated and miserable. For a Wabanaki, that is worse than death; we are a tribe — it's the most important thing." Elias was unsure and waited for more. "I'm sad to say, that is the way of the world. And your children, you must think of them."

"What about them?"

"They would be mixed. In the English world, half-breed. You know this."

"No, Marguerite, people will love Owaissa — just as I do!"

"No, Elias, you would find yourself distanced from your community, even your own family, unable to be part of either culture." Elias still listened; Marguerite was making some sense, but he hoped she would say differently. "Elias, the rest of the world is not like ours — we accept each other, marry each other — trappers and French and Algonquin — even sometimes

English — because of love. But that is here. If you go to your colony, you will have an unhappy wife, and because of it, you will be unhappy too." Marguerite left Elias and moved another bunch of corn closer to her work area. She turned back and watched Elias for long moments while he poked at the fire with another stick.

"Look my friend, if you want Owaissa, if you love her, and I don't doubt that you do, and you want to build a life with her, you need to do it here — in Owaissa's world." The silence stretched until Elias finally spoke.

"Do you think your tribe, the people would accept me?"

"Accept you? We love you, Elias!" Marguerite moved to hug Elias. "You can live here — as I have done. It will be wonderful! You can even move in with us if you like."

Marguerite's longhouse was big enough, but could he give up his life in Lancaster? A year ago, it would have been unthinkable. But everything had changed. Marguerite let the matter resolve itself and did not get too involved. Elias was quiet too before he finally stood to leave.

"Thank you," he mumbled, moving closer to accept another embrace. "That settles it then." But it did not settle anything; it made it worse. He prayed for strength because now the big problem was what to do about Atonwa — and a deadly fight that would probably have to come.

THIRTY-SIX

S UMMER WAS OVER, the leaves were falling and Elias was thinking about harvest time at home. He was finished teaching the operation of the mill. Now he had no time to lose as he hurried to see the French administrator attached to Governor Vaudreuil's office. It was time to discuss the next steps. After the doorman led him to the assistant for the governor's aide, the attendant announced,

"Robert de Poitier Sieur de Buisson is available now to see you."

"My work here is done, Sir. I am ready to leave."

"Oui, Monsieur, Sawyer. I have been instructed to arrange your departure as soon as possible. We have your payment ready as promised along with a guard to escort you to Lake Champlain. You should be safe from there to journey to your home."

"Thank you, Monsieur. I appreciate the arrangements. I still have a few people to say goodbye to, but I should be ready by week's end."

"Fine, that should give you plenty of time to gather souvenirs to bring home. I trust you will visit some of our shops for presents and souvenirs?"

"Good idea," said Elias. He had not thought much about gifts. But he should bring a surprise for his mother and some Algonquin things for his nieces and nephews. For that he would need Marguerite and Owaissa to help.

After a few days, Elias had finalized plans. It was time to talk to Owaissa. Marguerite had sent an invitation to meet for a meal at her lodge, and when Owaissa arrived, they ate and talked like they always did. But Elias could tell she sensed tension; something must have been different about the way he was acting. When they finished eating, Elias led her through the wigwam opening into the cold air outside.

"Owaissa...I was talking to Marguerite, and she said, I mean, I was wondering — I thought if you wanted to, that is, maybe you and I, we could talk about, you know — maybe getting married someday?" Owaissa let Elias stammer along until he had finished, then turned to kiss him.

"I would like to marry you, Elias, yes, very much. But are you sure that's what you want — to marry an Algonquin girl?" Elias started to explain what he had planned — how he was never more sure of anything — how he wanted to spend all his days with her. But as he started to speak, he swallowed her in his arms instead, kissing her mouth and then her ear. "I want to live my life with you, Owaissa."

"Where will we live? I think I may be afraid to live in your Lancaster."

"Well, no, I mean yes, I want to live here — like Marguerite and others like her have done. I want to be one of your people."

Owaissa's look was intent, as if to judge the unspoken, possibly measuring Elias's sincerity. Elias felt awkward and began to notice how cold the air was as he waited for Owaissa to respond.

"You have given this thought? You have talked to others?"

"Yes, I have, I have thought about it. I want to have a family with you — here in your land."

"What about your English people? Your father? Your mother?" Elias was ready for the question.

"They will understand — once I tell them about you. My father always wants what's best for me. And my mother, she will understand too." It was enough explanation, but he went on. "As for others, I don't care. They do not know what it's like living here. They could never understand. I am going home to tell them my plans — about you — us. If I leave now, I can return soon after the snow melts; we can marry then." Elias explained everything, but when he had finished, Owaissa did not speak, as if she was waiting for what Elias had not said. Then she spoke.

"Maybe I should go with you?"

"No, it's a long journey. It's only about seven moons until the ice melts, and the snow is gone. Then I'll be back. I want to see my parents and tell them the good news. You can tell your family so everyone will be ready. We can have a big party, qu' est ce que c'est la grande ball?' We'll invite everyone — even Governor Vaudreuil!"

Owaissa was considering, although she was not as eager as Elias had expected. She had turned her back with her chin tucked low, snuggled near her chest.

"What's wrong, Owaissa? I thought you would be happier

about everything. Aren't you sure about being an Englishman's wife?"

"Oh, no, it's not that. I am looking forward to learning more English — and teaching you better French. But I am afraid I will never see you again, that is all. What if you do not return?" Elias did not respond. "It sounds like such a long way, and it will be a long time." Elias spun her around and pulled her close.

"Owaissa, I am certain God sent me here to find you, and there's nothing I won't do to be with you. I have loved you from the moment I saw you outside Marguerite's lodge. I'll be back; you just have to trust me."

"I do, Elias." Owaissa's face was close to his. "I do trust you. But I do not want to stay and wait. I will go with you. We could live in your Lancaster, no?"

"No, Owaissa. You do not know the white man's heart. There are many who are good — like my family. But many are not. They do not try to understand people who are different. They want everyone to be the same as they are." Elias had hoped it was not going to be this difficult.

"Do you understand?"

"Your people would not accept me? Is that what you are saying? Because I am Algonquin? I am not of your religion?"

"No. I mean yes, a little. But it's only because they don't know you — not the way I do, that's all. It's not you." That had little effect, so Elias pressed on. "We don't mix. And our children — you know how mean children can be. White folks look down on mixed breeds. I love your family and your ways. We can have a good life here. You'll see." Owaissa crushed herself against his arm as they began to walk.

"There is another thing," said Elias.

"What's that?"

"Atonwa."

"What about him?"

"He is not happy about us. I mean, it's just that he wants you for himself."

"For himself?" Owaissa let out a grunt. "I would never marry him. We were friends when we were small, but now he is so full of himself. And ugly! Thinks he's going to be chief someday."

"But even if he is a little ugly, he could still make you happy, no?"

"You are teasing now, Elias. I can tell. I do not like Atonwa — not at all. He is too big a boaster. He will have to find another. I love you."

"I'm worried. When I'm gone, he will come for you. I am sure of that."

"He better not! My father said I can choose whom to marry — and when. So, I will wait for you. I promise!"

They hurried back to share their news with Marguerite and then moved on to Owaissa's parents' longhouse. Everyone was excited, although not too surprised. What did surprise them was that Elias would live as a Mississaugas with more questions about his planned return to Lancaster first. Owaissa's mother hugged and kissed her daughter along with a long hug for her soon-to-be-son-in-law. Owaissa's father was especially happy as he announced with a loud boast,

"Elias, I welcome you into our tribe!" When the evening ended, Elias floated back toward his lodge with a full stomach and thoughts mixed with preparations for the difficult trip home and delicious dreams of nights with Owaissa.

He was pleased with himself; he had not revealed his entire plan — how he would say his family goodbyes, but also something more important. He imagined ramming cotton wadding and a perfect ball down the barrel of a heavy, new musket. His father had taught him what a musket meant in this life, and Elias embraced the feelings that rose inside — the relief he would feel in being armed again — the power — the comfort the weapon lying beside him would provide as he slipped into sleep.

When he returned for Owaissa, he would be ready to meet Atonwa. But this time his opponent would find a surprise — not the frightened prisoner he had been, but a confident, free man — with a musket. And when it was over, he would pray to Owaissa's God for forgiveness — and to his own.

THIRTY-SEVEN

O WAISSA'S FATHER EXPLAINED the plan, and the family prepared a big send-off.

"Joachim and Wematin will guide you to Lake Champlain. Our people there will continue to guide you, following the rivers as far south as possible. Awasos is going too. He will secure a guide to take you east as close to your English settlements as possible. It will be dangerous near the English, so you will need to be careful. Our spirit will travel with you, Elias. You are a son to me now. Return quickly. Go now. Owaissa will walk you to the beginning of the path."

Owaissa and Elias eased away from the lodge, and when they were alone, Owaissa produced a surprise.

"I've made something for you." Owaissa handed Elias a package enclosed in a deerskin wrapper. When he unraveled it, he found a medallion with the image of a pinecone on a rawhide string. Wear this always to help you think of me. It was my grandmother's — she gave it to me before she died." Elias slipped it over his head and leaned lower to kiss Owaissa while she pressed against him.

"Thank you. I will not take it off until I am back with you. I better go now; the braves are waiting."

Owaissa grabbed his arm. "Wait! One more thing. I made this for you as well." She reached in her bag and produced a thicker package. Elias unwrapped a reddish-brown earthen plate. Owaissa giggled as she watched Elias's turning it over, inspecting the gift as if savoring the feel before she added a wish. "With it, no harm can reach you."

"This is beautiful, Owaissa. I hope I can carry it without breaking it. How did you make it?"

"Marguerite helped. We formed it, then fired it in the oven. It is my first, so not exactly perfect. See here, where it is supposed to be round? It came out a little uneven."

"No, it's nice. Here, let me put it under the beaver skins so it doesn't get broken on the way back." When he had packed the plate, they hugged for a long time, neither one saying a word. He could hear her breathing, her grip as strong as it had ever been.

"Please be safe," Owaissa whispered, beginning to cry. "And come back to me soon."

"I will, Owaissa — soon. I promise! And you better be waiting when I get back!" He tried to joke, but Owaissa's eyes were filled. "I'll be back when the air is the hottest, and the grass long. When the leaves fall again, we will be together." Elias lifted her chin. "I will think of you every day. Please, Owaissa, don't cry."

With that, he pulled away, lifting his pack and hatchet. He trotted to the edge of the woods before turning for a last look back. Owaissa had settled to a sitting position with her chin on her chest and her shoulders shaking as she cried.

THIRTY-EIGHT

E LIAS LEFT CANADA, his home for almost two years, with several escorts. After two days, all but Awasos turned back. They traveled south, walking along the banks of the Chambly River to the shore of Lake Champlain. There they met other Wabanaki braves who provided two canoes and another guide who continued to the headwaters of the lake where they left the canoes. In a few days, Elias thought the air felt warmer as a sense of home began to stir in him. Unlike the attack and cruel remove, this travel was more leisurely with building excitement of getting home.

The forest was dark under a thick canopy of fat, full hemlock, giant pine and leafy trees — oaks, maples and elm. The trail was almost imperceptible as it wound through the underbrush, crossing streams and smaller rivers that sliced through the woods. In most places, visibility was no more than twenty feet with thick underbrush as they continued southeast. Elias thought if things went right, he would be hugging his mother soon.

There was little conversation with his lone companion and little sound in the woods until with the blast of exploding powder, the stillness was shattered with tree bark snapped near Elias's head, throwing a sharp piece of wood against his cheek. Before he could realize what had happened, more bark pieces flew with the crack of many muskets and a thundering volley of shots.

"Down!" he yelled, to his guide. The warning was not necessary — the brave was already pressed flat on the forest floor, crawling toward a fallen log. Elias rolled and began to crawl for better cover as well, while lead balls slapped through the trees, shattering wood, sending down a shower of leaf parts and pieces of tree branches. As the lead balls smacked into the trees, Elias and his guide traded astonished, frightened looks while pressing themselves tighter against the spongy moss and dead leaves covering the ground. Elias was ashamed of his carelessness, never suspecting they would meet a militia this far from a settlement. But it was too late. What should have been a joyous reunion had turned deadly. He recognized the terror in his young guide's eyes.

"Go!" Elias gestured with his hands and fingers, hoping the young brave would understand and crawl away. "Go back, go back!" When the shooting abated a bit, Elias shouted his loudest. "Hold up!" His cry only caused another flurry of gunshots. "Hold up! Hold Up! English! I am English!" The shooting began to diminish to a few occasional shots. "I am English," he shouted in the growing silence. Then after a few moments, an English voice responded.

"Move out where we can see you, Indian. Show your

hands!" Elias signaled for his guide again who still had not moved, pointing for him to crawl away. "Go, Guide, back. Go home!" The guide hesitated for moments, but as Elias coaxed, the brave crawled several feet, stopping behind another thick tree, then another. When Elias gestured again, the guide finally signaled a goodbye. Only then did Elias stand, still hidden behind the tree.

"I'm coming out! Don't shoot! I'm English. I have no weapon." When he had eased himself from behind the big pine, a musket snapped before a ball smacked the tree bark a few feet above his head.

"Heathen! If I see you move, or if you got more friends in the woods, you are a dead Indian. On the ground! Are you alone?"

"Yes, yes! I am Elias Sawyer. From Lancaster! Two years captive in Canada. Just released. I have no musket!" The forest was quiet before a calmer voice responded.

"Alright, stand up where we can see you. Move a little closer — nice and easy-like. This better not be a trick."

As Elias moved closer, several men, then several more, emerged from their cover. They looked like soldiers, each wearing a similar-looking shirt.

"I am Captain Shaw, and this here is the Haverhill Militia. We come up following the Merrimack River. I do not know why you're out here wandering around, young man, dressed like that, but you must not like living too much. We got word there is another raid coming any time. These woods are crawling with the devils. You look just like one of 'em."

"Tarnation, look Captain," said one of the soldiers. "He's even got a feather on!"

Elias's ponytail hung below his shoulders, his moccasins and deerskin pants were well-worn with his shirt adorned with bright colored beads. The captain looked to be considering Elias's appearance and then offered advice with a shaking head.

"Son, if I didn't know better, I'd think you were a little crazy. People around here are mighty scared and awful jumpy. If you keep slinking around looking like that, you are gonna get yourself killed. You look like a damned savage." As the captain talked, Elias made eye contact with each of the dozen, eager men who surrounded him.

"Where are your provisions Son? Not even a pack?"

"It's in the bushes. I had help but when you started shooting, I lost my guide. I signaled him to run. He means you no harm. Don't worry, he's long gone."

"Sergeant, take two men and go check out his story. Something does not smell right. Be careful."

Elias called after the soldiers as they moved away. "Careful with my pack!"

The captain turned from Elias and removed his hat. After running his fingers through his thick hair, he turned back to Elias.

"I figure you might be one of the luckiest men I've ever met. If I'm right, you just may have an interesting story to tell. We can sit and eat while we hear it. You hungry?" The soldiers settled in the shade at the edge of the clearing where they shared food, and Elias watched wonder creep across the men's faces as he let his story out.

******

CAPTAIN SHAW DETAILED three soldiers to accompany Elias for the next few days to follow the Merrimack River south to the settlement of Pawtucket where the Concord River meets — then on to Concord, arriving just before sunset. Like Lancaster, the Concord land had also been purchased from the Indians and for several years before Lancaster was the furthest western outpost in the Bay Colony. Elias had traveled thirty-seven days. Now he was one day's ride from home. The final leg would be easy with a horse he purchased with some of the gold pieces Father Andre provided as payment for his service. He planned to follow the only trail west — the narrow cart path built by his grandfather's generation to connect Lancaster with Cambridge and the seacoast. The ride would be flat and easy, except for the difficult crossing at the Sudbury River.

Leaving Concord later in the day than he had planned, he did not arrive at the Sudbury River until noon where he dismounted and removed his moccasins and pants before swimming his horse across. He held the roan's mane and floated alongside the horse's neck to give him the best chance of swimming. He remounted and followed the trail west, fighting desire to gallop the horse. *I'm so close to home!* But he kept his emotion bottled, enjoying the ride along the clear path.

Near the top of Wataquadock Hill, he reined in his horse. While the animal snapped at the tall grass on the edge of the path, Elias absorbed the view. He had forgotten how beautiful the horizon looked from the high vantage point that provided the Mt. Wachusett profile rising with a dark, green form on a palette of color that blazed in the bed of New England trees. After such a long time, the view was even better than he'd remembered.

The ride had taken longer than he had expected; the sun had already dipped below the trees. By the time he passed the meeting house on Wilder Road, it was almost dark. He did not need Captain Shaw's caution to know it would not be wise to enter the town this late. He would get himself shot. *What a pity, killed by a neighbor, after all I have been through!* When Elias stopped and settled for the night, he wrapped a soft band around the horse's front legs to allow him to graze without wandering too far. Elias moved into a stand of pines, cleared a patch and started a small fire. He was not cold or planning to cook, but he wanted the fire for company, enjoying the crackling wood, listening as the burning pieces snapped and popped.

The woods were still. When the moon came up, an owl broke the quiet with a call, *who-who...who, who, huh who...* The sky was cloudless, lit by a thousand stars. Elias knew the North Star — every young settler learned that, along with Orion's belt and the Big Dipper. He wondered if Owaissa might be looking at the stars at that moment as well. As he began to drift to sleep, his last thoughts were imagining her skin touching his, listening to her breathing while they lay awake enjoying the night sky.

THIRTY-NINE

E LIAS WOKE WITH the first hint of light and prepared for the last leg of his two-year adventure. When he mounted, his horse's steps quickened as if the animal might have smelled other horses or sensed the ride's end. They dropped from the high ground, moving closer to the Nashua River where the south branch slid in gently from the west to join the north branch where his grandfather and others began the Lancaster settlement in the valley — ten miles long — eight miles wide.

Elias was weary, but propelled by soaring spirits as the horse followed the trail into the village. The morning was fall cold with a thin plume of smoke lifting from each house that lined the lane in neat rows. Their capture felt like a lifetime ago, and he noticed more houses than he remembered. An unexpected sense of peace settled over him as he recognized the houses and the families who lived in each. *Atherton, Gates, Joslin, Fairbanks, with seven children — Whitcomb — five children when he had left.* He knew them all. *There's Widow*

Hanson's place; she must be remarried by now.

A boy was the first to notice.

"Father look!" he shouted. "A rider!" It was not long before another shout, and others reacted. Doors opened. Men appeared with muskets. Women appeared in doorways. Two boys loped alongside, close enough as if for a better look and to touch the horse.

"Hey, mister," another boy hollered as he ran near the horse's legs. "Can I pet your horse?" When Elias stopped, more boys joined, followed by sisters and brothers. People appeared from everywhere, examining his horse while Elias sat back in the saddle enjoying the welcome.

There was order to the settlement he had forgotten, the houses even and square as if made with a common plan, arranged neatly like biscuits in a pan. The evenly-spaced windows were similar in size, and the warm smell of wood smoke saturated the air. His heart pounded, anticipating walking across the threshold into his mother's kitchen before lifting her with his biggest hug. Seeing his father again, after what they had gone through together, would be more joyous than he could imagine. He hoped his father's journey home a year ago had been an easy one.

The crowd swelled around him. Elias knew he must be an interesting-looking stranger, appearing more like an Indian than a white man. His pants were deerskin, and he wore moccasins. His shirt was a loose-fitting deerskin pullover with Owaissa's medallion hung in front. His face was smooth like an Indian's, his hair pulled back in a long ponytail — a beaded headband squeezed across his forehead that held a white feather that hung on the back of his head. Across the flanks of his horse, rested two heavy-looking packs with beaver hides bulging out.

"Where you from, Fella?" Elias recognized Harry Tracy, a friend of his father. "You sure aren't from these parts."

"You been traveling far?" another asked. Elias let the people look him over before he finally spoke.

"Yes, I have," he answered in a tired voice. "A very long way." He waited to savor the moment before letting the rest out. "But I'm home, now." He urged his horse to pick its way along the path to the Sawyer garrison, the animal plowing through the people like a canoe.

"Where are you set to go?" Elias knew Robert Higman who often traded with his father, but the man did not recognize him. His wife, Martha, did and let everyone know.

"My God in heaven!" she shrieked. "It's Elias Sawyer. Is that really you?" Elias turned his head and tried to stop a smile, but the woman grabbed at his leg and shook it with delight. "It is you, Elias, isn't it? You can't fool me, boy! I was there with your mother the day you were born! I'd know you anywhere, even if you are a bit more grownup now with all that hair!" The woman took a breath and surveyed Elias. "My Lord, Elias, Lord have mercy! Wait until your mother sees you!"

Elias rode on until finally stopping in front of his house, dismounting and handing the reins to the first pair of hands that reached. As he eased his way to the front porch, his moccasins made no sound climbing the three wooden steps. When he tried the latch, the door creaked inward, letting morning light spill across his shoulders into the shadows. When his mother spun around toward the silhouette in the doorway, her hands moved to her mouth as if stifling a scream.

When Elias spoke, as tenderly as he could, his mother's hands slipped away from her mouth, her arms dropping to her sides as if with a life of their own.

"Hello, Mother. It's very good to see you." His mother covered her face and began to sob into her hands. Elias covered the distance and swallowed her into a smothering embrace. She was frail and thin — not as he remembered. Neither one said a word until her body stopped shaking, and her sobs quieted.

"Elias! Elias! Is this you — come home to me?"

"Yes, it's me, Mother."

"Lord, how can I thank you? My boy has come home! Elias, I have missed you more than you can know! Now look at your hair!" she shrieked. "You look like a wild man! A wild, Indian man!"

Elias hugged her again. He could almost lift her with one hand, so he held her tenderly.

"I have been dreaming of your cooking for two years! Now, what's for breakfast?"

"Let me start the bacon for you! Go get your father; he's at the barn. You go. I will make the best breakfast you have ever eaten. Hurry now!"

One of the neighbors had already run to deliver the news to Mr. Sawyer who was trotting toward the house, reaching the step just as Elias stepped out the front door.

"What's this now, a young native prowling around for a meal?" Elias did not speak but embraced his father with a strong clamp that lasted a long time until they eased their grasp for back slaps.

"Look at you, Father! You do not look a day older. This southern climate and millwork must agree with you!" Elias was lying; he thought his father had aged greatly. It was only partly the white in his father's hair. Elias thought his father's journey home at fifty-nine years must have been difficult. Or maybe Elias had just never noticed before.

"Yes, it does." Mr. Sawyer patted his stomach. "There's a lot to be said about home cooking!" While they ate, Elias's parents shared news about the community until they finished and the conversation began to wane. Elias took out the presents.

"Here you go, Mother. I had this made especially for you." He presented her a beaded bracelet, covered with yellow and turquoise shells. "Go ahead, put it on so we can see how it looks." Mrs. Sawyer lifted her arm, turning it one way, then another, as she admired her gift.

"This is the first jewelry I've gotten since we moved to Lancaster! Thank you, Elias. I love it!" For his father, Elias unpacked a deerskin shirt, offering it with a wide grin.

"I hope you like this, Father, it's my size, so if it doesn't fit, it can be mine." His father slipped the shirt over his head. The covering hung loosely with sleeves designed for activity, cut halfway down his forearms. The neck was open in a V.

"Elias, you won't be getting this back until I'm gone!"

"It's warm in the winter and cool in summer," Elias revealed more gifts: a hatchet for his father and more jewelry for his mother. "Here's a knife for you, Father. The handle is part of a moose antler. One of my friends showed me how to make it. It's my first one, but I think it came out pretty good. See, the scabbard has a little pocket to keep a wet stone or a flint." Elias pulled Owaissa's plate from the skins last, cradling it with special care as he told its story.

"It's made specially too. I worried about getting it home in one piece. "Can we keep it over the fireplace, Mother?"

"Of course, Elias, it will look lovely on the mantle. Don't worry, there will be no using it for meals either. I just love the color! It looks like one of a kind." Each time Elias looked at the plate, he thought of Owaissa — how she had cried when he had left. He wanted his parents to consider it an important reminder, but he did not want to go into all the rest — at least not yet.

FORTY

TWO DAYS LATER, the Sawyers had an important visitor dressed in black pants and shirt with a bright, white collar. It was the Reverend John Prentice.

"Mr. Sawyer! God has been good to your family. You must be extremely thankful to have your son finally home!"

"Reverend, you cannot know. I am the happiest man alive just to have my family back together. It was an extremely trying ordeal, but now we can finally put it all behind us."

"A test from our maker," replied the minister. "Have faith the Lord never gives us anything we cannot handle. We need to be confident in that, Mr. Sawyer. You are a living example for all to see."

Mrs. Sawyer offered warm cornbread she had prepared right from the coals.

"Come, Reverend, eat and tell us the news from the other churches in Boston and Concord."

"Well, I don't know where to start. Here, this may interest

you, especially with the circumstances of your husband and son's capture and all. I received a bill recently from Cotton Mather. He and the Governor are having quite the fight."

"Why is that?" asked Mr. Sawyer.

"Seems Reverend Mather is calling for Governor Dudley's removal. He has written a long piece detailing his grievances. Here, let me read some of it for you.

'I am accusing Dudley of profiting from illegal trade with the French and Indian enemies, failing to negotiate the return of captives or provide adequately for the colony's defense.'"

"I think he's right," said Mr. Sawyer. "It's not so much the Indians. Our soldiers must do something about the French. They are the ones stirring up the trouble. They have taken hundreds now and authorities in Boston don't seem focused enough on getting them back."

"That's what Cotton Mather says. Thinks we've been too easy on the French. Everyone knows they are behind the kidnappings. Maybe when France and England finish fighting, the attacks and kidnappings will finally stop. We have certainly seen a lot of people murdered or captured. Or worse." Then the minister changed his attention.

"Elias, did you come across other white captives in Canada?"

"Yes, Reverend, I did; there were quite a few."

"How are they treated — like slaves, I'd imagine?"

"No, Reverend, that wasn't so. Those I saw were treated very well — like members of the tribe. I was surprised. They came to like living with the Indians — especially the children."

"It's interesting you say that," replied the minister. "There have been numerous reports indicating that very thing. Reverend Williams of Deerfield has been unsuccessful in negotiating the return of his daughter, Eunice. He's traveled there twice, but despite numerous overtures, the child is still not redeemed."

"Can you even imagine?" Mrs. Sawyer groaned the words. "God help us."

Elias had things he would like to say but found himself beginning to choose his words carefully.

"There is a lot of intermarriage in Canada between the Indians and the French. The trappers, that is. My friend, Marguerite, was captured years ago. She speaks French, and English now, along with Abenaki — several dialects too. Her husband is French — mixed with Missiquoi and Iroquois. They have three beautiful children and believe me, she is very happy.

"Well, that is a mystery. I cannot understand why a white woman would want to marry an Indian. And captured children turning Indian, I cannot understand that either. I suppose they are so impressionable. But a woman? That is different. I suspect she may have been compromised."

Elias was eager to answer. "People have never had the chance to live with the Indians. My grandfather told me about it. The first settlers cooperated, but not their children. Everything changed with the next generations — on both sides."

"Elias, it's not that simple" the minister began. "It is God's will — the way he intended it. This land was prepared for us, and Lancaster is the fruit of God's vision. Our Christian way of life, the world we have created is the Lord's design." Reverend Prentice looked satisfied he had done his work and had delivered his message well.

"Elias, I wanted to ask you, if you'd like to, that is. I wondered if you might like to speak to the congregation. Soon, I hope. The people are interested in your captivity and experiences living with the savages." Elias was not interested in doing anything like it but was nervous about refusing the minister. Reverend Prentice pressed on. "You might understand, you are quite a celebrity now. There are even a few brethren from Watertown and Cambridge who would like to come to hear you when you talk." The minister let his words sink in and looked at Elias's mother as if for help.

"That would be interesting, Elias," she said. "I'd love to hear more about your time in Canada too."

"Did you encounter Christians among the natives — other than the Jesuits?"

"All Catholics, Reverend. The Jesuits try hard, but the Wabanaki only go along to a point — more to humor the Fathers, I think. They will not accept the white man's faith. They have their religion."

"Yes, well, they are bound to pagan worship, I suppose. That's only natural. I think our English clergy could do a better job if we could get rid of the French. Our missionaries have had some success with the praying Indians in Massachusetts Bay. We do have some Christian Indians."

"Reverend, I was surprised about the Indians' beliefs. They don't worship as we do."

"So, Elias, I'd hoped you would tell us how the Lord empowered you through your ordeal. It would be wonderful to hear about your journey and more about how the Indians and French live — how you prayed and what gave you strength in your times of distress. Could we plan on next Sunday?" Elias agreed only that he would try to gather his thoughts and come up with something that might interest the congregation. Next Sunday would be too soon.

"I'll try, Reverend. Maybe later, if that's all right."

"Good, good! That's fine. Certainly, whenever you are ready. I will make an announcement. The people will be so thrilled!" When the Reverend was ready to leave, he asked the family to bow their heads to pray.

"Lord, thank you for your bountiful blessings for the Sawyers, in bringing Elias and Thomas home safely to remain with us. And thank you for continuing to protect all Lancaster families from those the devil sets upon us. We pray the conflicts will end soon, and we can carry out your plan for this land. In Jesus' name, we pray. Amen."

When the "amens" had been said, and the minister left, Elias moved outside. The sun had slipped below the tree line, and twilight lit the countryside in soft, pink light. He walked down the slope from the back of the house to the edge of the Nashua River, shuffling through leaves that covered the trail. Fall was at its peak, with trees blazing in spectacular reds and crimsons, yellow and orange shades. The bright yellow birch leaves were just starting to fall, and a few maple leaves had begun dropping with each new gust of wind. Elias enjoyed the fall air with the crisp absence of humidity, and best of all, no mosquitoes. When he found the special log, he sat, remembering how he and his grandfather had often done the same.

The trees along the bank had been spared the saw, leaving the river looking the way it had before the first settlers came. The water was dark and peaceful, the river oozing with a slow push of water. As a boy, he had been able to throw a rock across to the opposite bank, and his grandfather taught him to fish here.

He was sad he had missed saying goodbye to his grandfather who had died while he was in Canada. If only he could have brought Owaissa to meet him; he would have loved her. Elias also recognized a surprising new feeling, a stirring he could never share with anyone, especially his parents. He could almost envision the native people who lived here before his grandfather's generation came. There had surely been Joachims and Lazars — even an angry Atonwa. He had new feelings — this place was not his or even his grandfather's but the home of the people who came before. He felt the spirit of the original people, and his heart told him his Lancaster friends and neighbors were living on land that did not belong to them.

FORTY-ONE

A LETTER FROM Boston notified the Sawyers of the Massachusetts Bay Militia's pending visit. Eighteen riders arrived just after noon, moving down the road before stopping at the Fairbank's house and asking for the Sawyer garrison. As the lieutenant climbed the steps of the Sawyers' porch, the soldiers watered their horses in the communal trough before settling in the shade of two towering elm trees.

"Hello, you must be Mr. Sawyer. I am Lieutenant Mosley from Boston. Major Kelly sent us."

"Come in Lieutenant," replied Mr. Sawyer. "Get out of the hot sun. We've been expecting you."

The lieutenant leaned his neck to lower his head and stooped to clear the door. He held his hat as he crossed the room to the table. He was unusually tall with a trimmed beard and neatly cut black hair. He wore a pistol strapped to his waist with pants tucked into a pair of high, black, leather riding boots. On each jacket shoulder, a patch indicated his rank and affiliation. The soldiers outside were dressed the same, and Elias noticed hanging from each of the horses' black saddles, a long musket.

"Please, Lieutenant," offered Mrs. Sawyer. "Have some apple cider. It's freshly made."

"Thank you, Ma'am. This must be Elias. I've heard so much about him."

Mr. Sawyer reached for the lieutenant's hand then waited for their visitor to drink his cider. When the soldier set the half-empty glass on the table, Thomas spoke.

"Yes, this is my son, Elias, Lieutenant. Did you travel from Concord this morning?"

"Yes, we left at first light. I have never been this far west before, and I must say, it was a pleasant trip." The lieutenant paused to reach again for his drink. "This is certainly a beautiful country. But I'm not planning an overnight; it's much too dangerous. We'll be leaving straight away."

"Yes, Lieutenant, we have had our difficulties."

"I'm a little surprised at your settlement though. I am not sure what I had expected, but it's very established — and orderly. It looks as if you have been busy."

"Yes, Lieutenant, this settlement has been here a long while. Lancaster was started not too long after Plymouth Plantation. We've over one hundred families now — eleven garrison houses."

"Well, that brings me to the purpose of my visit. Governor Dudley mandated we bolster protection for outlying communities in the Massachusetts Bay from French and Indian attacks. You see I have brought a contingent of men. We plan to billet one man in each of your garrison houses. Your families will be responsible for feeding and making sure our men have proper accommodations." Lieutenant Mosley drank the last of his cider and then addressed Elias.

"Young man, I have heard about your captivity and remove. It must have been a trying ordeal."

"It wasn't that bad, Sir. All in all, I was treated very well."

"You met with Governor Vaudreuil, I presume, especially right before your release?"

"Yes, I did — I met with him a few times."

"Part of my mission is to meet with you, Elias. My superior, Captain Kelly, the commander of Militia, thought it wise to ask for your help." Elias waited for the lieutenant to explain. "Did the governor share with you any of his plans — possibly mention any English settlements by name?"

"No, we never talked about that — just the mill and my work and other things."

"Did anyone else you met ever talk about the attacks?" Elias was unsure of how to respond and was beginning to feel a little trapped. He looked at his father for reassurance, but Mr. Sawyer was waiting as well.

"Occasionally someone would mention a raid, but that was as far as it went. The braves were away a lot, and they did not include me in any discussions. I never knew much about what might be going on." The lieutenant was disappointed but acted satisfied with Elias's response.

"Well, it was certainly worth a try. We have been receiving hints for months about a planned attack. The reports are from various sources. Something is brewing, and we suspect it might be a big one. We just don't know where — or when." Elias's mother moved closer.

"Oh, my, Lieutenant, do you think it could be Lancaster?"

"It could be, Ma'am; it's the easiest target, but it's impossible to say and difficult to protect so many towns. The attack could come before winter — anytime — anywhere. Is there anything you can share with us Elias that might provide us assistance? Any information could prove helpful."

Elias remembered conversations with Marguerite and what Joachim had revealed. That would not help, so he decided not to share. But the idea of an attack began to bother him in new ways. He thought of his friends — how excited they had been about joining their first raid and about Atonwa. He did not doubt Atonwa could kill in the worst ways possible. Lazar had been killed and as for Joachim and the others, he worried what kind of danger his friends might his face or what they might do. He had not thought about possibilities in this way. Now that he was back in Lancaster, things were different — *everything was confusing; if only there could be peace.*

Mr. Sawyer sounded worried when he asked about a possible raid.

"Lieutenant, judging by what you're telling us, a lot of people may be involved — possibly much killing on both sides."

"That's right, Mr. Sawyer. That's why we want to be aggressive with this situation. Part of the problem is the tribe in Arcadia. The Abenaki are allied with the French. It's Governor Vaudreuil in Québec, he's the problem. He uses the Algonquins to do his fighting."

"It's a cowardly way to fight," said Mr. Sawyer.

"That may be cowardly from our perspective, Mr. Sawyer, but the French have their motives, and, from their point of view, until now it's been effective." The Lieutenant asked Mrs.

Sawyer for a glass of water as he glanced outside.

"Folks, I'm not afraid to tell you this; we are assembling a force of twenty ships with over one thousand men for a campaign. Militias are assembling from all over New England, including Rhode Island and New Hampshire. We are going to eliminate the stronghold of Port Royal."

"Nova Scotia?" Mrs. Sawyer asked.

"That's right, Ma'am."

"The land of the dawn,'" said Elias, surprising his parents and Lieutenant Mosely. "That's what my friends call it."

"See Elias," the lieutenant laughed. "You did pick up a lot while in Canada. It is still their base of operations in the northeast. Major Kelly will lead the operation. Until we capture it, their attacks will continue. Once Arcadia is secure, we will turn our sights on Quebec. That's the real rats' nest. It's Chief Grey Cloud and a few others. And the scheming French governor. They are all in it together."

"Is Major Church still running things?" Mr. Sawyer asked.

"No, but we wish he were. Unfortunately, he has retired. You're right, he would have had things mopped up by now with someone's head on a pole."

"That's horrible," said Mrs. Sawyer.

"It may be, but these are difficult times, Ma'am. I will admit, say what you want about his tactics, but Benjamin Church was effective." The lieutenant had warmed to the subject and began to elaborate. "Before you were born, Elias, when the Indians burned Lancaster, Major Church chased them all over Massachusetts Bay, finally cornering Phillip in a swamp in Rhode Island. One of his people gave the chief up. When they had finally killed Phillip, the soldiers quartered his body, and

Church had the chief's head mounted on a pole on Plymouth common — a message for all to see. It may still be there. Major Church knew how to fight Indians. He attacked villages up and down the frontier, and cleaned out a big encampment near here."

"That's right, Lieutenant," replied Mr. Sawyer. "Not far — at Waushakum. Soldiers killed about thirty people."

Mrs. Sawyer spoke up. "The story goes it was mostly women and children — and a few old men."

"Well, I'm afraid sometimes that's what it takes to finish things," replied the lieutenant. He paused, realizing who he was addressing. "But I don't need to tell you that, now do I?"

"I suppose not, Lieutenant." Mrs. Sawyer moved closer with the cider.

"Would you like more, Lieutenant?"

"No thank you, Ma'am, but you may remember I had two reasons for my visit." The lieutenant directed his comment to Mr. Sawyer as if there was no one else in the room.

"Mr. Sawyer, we would like Elias to come with us for this campaign — to join the militia. He's old enough, and he would be a tremendous help to us. He could…." Mrs. Sawyer let out a gasp, and the plate she was drying crashed to the floor.

"Oh, I'm so sorry," she mumbled as Elias moved to help her in gathering up the broken pieces. Mr. Sawyer responded with no attempt at remaining polite,

"Elias is no more than a boy, Lieutenant. He's not ready for Indian fighting."

"Please, Mr. Sawyer, let me explain. Elias would not need to enlist like a regular soldier. We were thinking along the lines of an interpreter — even a scout too. Elias, you know the terrain and after two years, I assume you understand the language, right?"

"Yes, some."

"Mr. Sawyer, Elias would be rewarded handsomely for his expertise." Lieutenant Mosley looked at Elias to gain his attention, and when their eyes locked, the lieutenant spoke directly to him.

"How do you feel about it, Elias — becoming an interpreter and scout for us? I can assure you and your family I will see to it you will not be put in harm's way — strictly behind the front lines — an advisor."

"He's too young." Mr. Sawyer sounded angry and stood up as if looking for an excuse to move about the room. He settled on a cup of water from the wooden bucket before facing Lieutenant Mosley.

"Lieutenant, we appreciate your help and concern for our homes, but Elias isn't going anywhere. We need him right where he is. We have plenty of work, and I'm not as young as I used to be. There are probably plenty of young men who would be eager to sign up for your campaign."

Lieutenant Mosley was apologetic and appeared resigned to accept Mr. Sawyer's argument. Elias looked at his father, then at his mother, and when his eyes met the lieutenant's, Elias shook his head.

"I'm sorry Sir. I don't think that would be such a good idea. My parents need me. There is so much to do here. We have a business." The lieutenant waited for more from Elias, but when nothing came, he sighed and pressed his hands on his calves, then rocked forward and stood, reaching for his hat on another chair.

"Well folks, my men are getting restless, and we have a long way to ride to get back before dark. I appreciate your hospitality. And please, do be vigilant. Tell your neighbors too. Lancaster is one of the Indians' favorite places to hit. Unless I am mistaken, you haven't seen the last of them."

"Thank you, Lieutenant. That is good advice, but not something I have to pass along. Our people are much aware of the dangers and have been on guard — ever since I was a boy. My generation has grown up with a threat of Indian attack." The Sawyers stood together waiting for the lieutenant's parting words.

"Folks, you can be sure of this. We are determined to stamp out the Indian problem. The authorities have even increased the bounty on Indian scalps to sixty dollars. Arcadia is the key. In the meantime, we are discouraging any non-essential travel until further notice. It's just too dangerous." The lieutenant thanked the Sawyers and began his departure with a "God speed."

Elias eased out of the house and made his way to the group of soldiers. He wanted to speak with the lieutenant without his parents.

"Lieutenant? Could I talk with you a bit more? I mean about scouting?"

"Certainly." He and Elias moved away from the other men. "Have you reconsidered my offer?"

"Well, not exactly, but I did want to ask where you are planning to go? I mean, how far north?"

"I'm not entirely sure. It all depends on what we encounter." Lieutenant Mosley studied Elias as if looking for an advantage in their discussion that might help him secure the young man as a recruit. "What's on your mind, Son?"

"If I could maybe go with you, for part of the way at least, then I could go on ahead." The lieutenant considered Elias's offer as if trying to understand his motive.

"Go on ahead? On ahead where?"

"To the Chambly."

"Why Chambly?" The lieutenant wanted the entire story now.

"That's where we built the mill. I have friends there. I'd like to get back to see them, that's all."

"Friends? What kinds of friends, Son? You do know we are at war with France, don't you?"

Elias felt exposed and ashamed of his attempt. Now cornered, he realized the only path forward was the entire truth.

"There's a girl. She is one of the Missiquoi Indians that live in the village by the rapids at Sault St. Louis — near the Mission du Sault St. Louis. That's where many of the Abenaki live."

"Lord have Mercy!" Lieutenant Mosley removed his hat and stroked back his black hair, then after he'd replaced his hat, he looked as though he could hardly contain himself. "You are telling me you want to travel with us for a piece, then go on alone, into the most dangerous country in the world — to see an Indian girl?" The lieutenant calmed himself and then spoke slowly, letting his words sink in while he watched for Elias's reaction.

"Elias, listen to me, Son. I think you should consider what you are saying. I am going to forget we ever talked about this. And I suggest you do the same." The lieutenant signaled one of the soldiers who led one of the horses close. When he had mounted, the horse spun as if to move before the lieutenant reined him to face Elias.

"Good luck, Son. If you should change your mind about joining us, be sure to let me know." He let the horse spin in a half-turn but stopped him to deliver one last comment.

"One more thing, Elias. I suggest you forget about whatever you left in Canada. The world is changing, and things are more dangerous now than ever. It's just not worth the risk."

When the soldier kicked his horse who began trotting up the rise past the houses, his words were still stinging as Elias watched. The soldiers followed before they all turned their horses at the opening to the path that led back to Concord.

FORTY-TWO

A S SUMMER SLID into late August, the men and boys brought hundreds of pumpkins from the fields. When another reminder came from Reverend Prentice about addressing the congregation, Elias figured he had run as long as possible, and it was time to come up with something to say.

"Today we have a special blessing," Reverend Prentice began. "God has worked in mysterious ways to provide us a wonder — a young man we all know who was wrenched from our midst by savages and thrown into the wilderness. Elias Sawyer faced no less a trial than Job, his redemption no less spectacular. It is now my pleasure to present and to join you in listening as he gives thanks for his return and shares some of his experiences living among the natives. Let me introduce Elias Sawyer — Lancaster's prodigal son!"

For Elias, it was uncomfortable in the crowded meeting-house, standing in front of his neighbors like a holy man with over one hundred people looking at him. As panic began to rise, he tried breathing slowly as Reverend Prentice had recommended, standing silently for a few long moments before beginning.

"Reverend Prentice asked me to speak to you today about my experiences in Canada, but I have been reluctant. Now before you, with my knees shaking, I remember why." The people laughed, and Elias felt better. "When the raiders surprised us in the mill that morning two years ago, at this same time of year with the morning air cold on our faces, just like today, I faced a fear like none before. But that fear doesn't compare with this!" Everyone laughed again, and the response helped ease Elias's nerves. He continued, haltingly at first, but as he warmed to his topic, he began to almost enjoy sharing his deeper thoughts for the first time. Memories continued to flood, helping to form words in his mind. When he thought his prepared talk lacking, he tried to let his emotions begin to control his comments.

"We have all been afraid in our lives. A boy is afraid of not measuring up in the eyes of his friends and family. I imagine a girl probably feels the same way, wondering how she looks, how she might marry someday — what kind of a mother she will be. Fathers are worried about how to feed their family and if they have made the right decisions about protecting them."

"And everyone fears God — because we know God punishes. When trouble comes, we wonder what we have done wrong. When we consider an action, we wonder how it will be perceived in God's eyes." Elias paused to enjoy a new feeling — that he had some important things to say before continuing with growing confidence. "But even greater is the fear of the Devil. Belief in God always carries with it belief in the Devil. It is the Devil and all his mysterious powers that drive us, coloring much of our behavior. It was fear of the Devil that created the witch trials we have learned about. We are here today to worship our God, but also, if we would be honest with ourselves, to shore up our walls with prayers, asking God to keep out the Devil." Elias took a drink of water from a tin cup to wet his throat.

"The biggest fear? This is what I learned as a result of my trial. The biggest of all, and we all have it, is the fear of each other — people who act or look the least bit different — people who do not eat or dress or talk like us — we fear. We fear the Catholics because of what they believe. We fear the French because they talk different — and do not worship like us. People with another religion, even though we may sing the same songs on meeting day, are feared most of all. Why? It's because they have a different God. And that is why we fear the Indians because they are the most different of all."

Elias stopped to look at the faces while trying to measure if his words were making sense. Since everyone remained still and quiet, he plowed ahead.

"You ask me to tell you of my experiences living in Canada — about the people — the French and the Indians. I was fortunate. You see, during it all — the attack, the remove to Quebec, the danger, I had hope. And it was not only my faith in God. It was simply this — my father was with me. Had I been alone, it would have been different."

Elias caught himself almost starting to cry and stopped to look down from the pulpit at his father who smiled, looking embarrassed, but nodding his head.

"I lived with the Wabanaki for two years, and I learned to

live without fear. The Indians have enemies, but they do not live in fear — not as we do. They embrace life, enjoying it in ways we could try to imitate. They find beauty in all things — the mountains and the trees and the rivers. I watched how they treat their children, teaching them to appreciate nature. And how the grandparents are revered — the most respected of the tribe. While the fathers are hunting to provide food, the grandparents spend time with the youth, teaching them the ways of the tribe, passing their culture down from generation to generation. I remember my times with my grandfather and wish there could have been more. I was looking forward to seeing him again, but God had another plan."

Elias stopped again to gauge if the people were still listening and if it was safe to talk of deeper things.

"The Indians teach their children there is a presence that can be found within all of us. When we reach for it, and begin to see ourselves as a part of what surrounds us, fear falls away, and we see our neighbors, and friends and family as a part of that as well."

When Reverend Prentice offered more water, Elias rested. No one moved. Even the children were still. Elias had spoken longer than he had intended, but the words had kept coming — thoughts that were in his heart — things he had not known were there. Then he finished in a slow gentle tone.

"Neighbors and friends, what I think I would most like to share with you is this — we are all the same — people with the same wants and desires, jealousies and aspirations. Some may wonder if I have 'gone native,' as it is said. But you need not worry. I am here. But I am surely different. I have returned to my family, and I am thankful for that. My joy abounds. I am thankful to be with you today and able to share what is in my heart."

When no more words came, Elias was finished. A hush remained within the meeting house. Reverend Prentice greeted him at the bottom step with an exuberant handshake before Elias returned to the pew with his mother and father. When he was seated, his father touched his leg, and Elias could not help noticing his mother wiping tears from her eyes.

As the service continued, the congregation sang, and Elias joined the minister in a walk to the door to prepare to greet each attendee as they left the meeting house.

"Great talk, Son!" Mr. Joslin said. "Enjoyed it very much."

"Thank you for sharing that, Elias," said Mrs. Parker. "It was interesting what you said about fear. You are right. We've all grown up with it."

The young boys hovered around Elias as if drinking in his look — the beaded headband, the moccasins and the deerskin britches. As Elias shook each adult's hand, he noticed the boys surveying him while whispering to each other in their little groups. Elias had never shaken so many hands and had begun to tire of it until one, female, was noticeably different — soft and warm as the young lady squeezed his. Her light brown hair had come loose on one side from under her bonnet, patting at her cheek. As she reached to brush it back, she dropped her gaze from Elias's in female demure.

"Hello," Elias said before she spoke.

"Hello," she responded, looking him square in his eyes. "It's nice to meet you. I'm Beatrix Houghton."

He was a little surprised he had never noticed her before — her pretty face shining from under the bill of her bonnet. As he thanked her, her eyes remained locked onto his.

"I enjoyed your talk," she said. "I did wonder about things — the Indians, that is. Do they have big families?" The line stopped, and people pushed past while others lingered, crushing closer to hear his responses.

"Not really, at least not as big as ours. Problem is, many of their children die when they are young. Over half. Maybe more." While Beatrix absorbed the information, it was only then that Elias realized he had not released her hand.

"We hope to see you again, Son," said the next man in line. "I'd like to hear more about the natives. And maybe you could teach my two boys how to be better hunters. I bet you have learned a lot!"

"I'd like to do that, Sir. Where do you live?"

"My place is just past Wheelers', next to the Houghtons. I'm Joshua Lewis. Come by when you get settled. You can try my new musket."

The woods of Lancaster were full of deer, and Elias was soon a popular companion for the Lewis boys and a few of their friends. He enjoyed talking about his time with the Indians, and the boys were interested in their ways — what young Indians did all day, what they wore if they played games or wrestled and fought with other tribes. Elias was pleased they were especially interested when he talked about the spirit in all things.

"The bear and raccoon and deer care for their offspring with the same love humans have for their offspring." He taught them to respect the animals and kill them with care and appreciation for the role they play in providing for their survival — what he learned from Lazar and the others. Elias talked about how the Great Spirit lives in all things like the trees and the river and especially Wachusett Mountain.

"There was a great tribe here once, you know, before our grandparents. In the beginning, they helped the settlers, but it was not long before our ancestors chased the tribes out. Can you try to imagine what that must have been like for the Indians — people whose families had lived here for generations to be driven away?"

And sometimes, when talking to the young people of Lancaster, Elias noticed he felt almost as much Abenaki as English.

FORTY-THREE

A FTER THE DAY spent at the mill, Elias's mother gave him the news.

"Elias, Samuel Naughton stopped by to invite us all for a meal next Sunday. He's planning to slaughter a pig."

When they arrived, Elias realized it was the home of Beatrix Houghton whom he had met at church weeks ago. He had not been back to church service since his talk. It did not feel right anymore; the sermon and prayers felt hollow. He was more spiritual when he was alone in the woods, walking along the banks of the Nashua River. From the top of Prospect Hill, a few miles to the east, he could sit and gaze on Mount Wachusett savoring its aura on the western horizon overlooking the green valley. He sometimes left the settlement in the late afternoon. It was not safe, he knew, but in the woods, he was not afraid.

His father said he understood and put no demands on him, and life was good. He fell back into the routine of Lancaster life — working at the mill in the morning — sometimes helping in the fields in the afternoon. As summer grew later, the Lancaster boys continued to seek him out, and Elias was busier than he had ever been. Lancaster was growing, and since people had to travel long distances to purchase cut boards, his father was planning another mill. He could not help noticing how interested the young women had become in what he had to say — and what two years had done with a few of his friends' sisters.

One morning, all the adults had left the garrison house, except Elias and his mother.

"Shouldn't you get down to the mill, Elias? Your father will be looking for you. Are you feeling all right?"

"I'm fine, Mother." His mother must have noticed Elias's stare because she stopped cleaning off the table and sat down close to wait for what he had to say.

"What is it, Elias?"

"I've been trying to decide how to tell you this," he started. "I didn't want to make you unhappy."

"Go ahead, Son. What could be so bad?"

"I've met someone, and I'm going to marry her."

"Oh, Elias, that's wonderful news! I knew it! I could tell by the way you have been acting. Let me guess; it's the Houghton girl?"

"No, Mother, it's a girl I left in Canada."

"Canada?"

"Yes, Mother. Owaissa is her name; she's a Wabanaki princess — from the Missoulu tribe. You would love her! She's beautiful!" He went on to tell his mother all about Owaissa — her hair, and how educated she was — how she spoke English and other languages. "She's waiting for me. She's the one who made me the red plate." Mrs. Sawyer listened quietly until Elias had finished.

"Why didn't you bring her back with you then?"

"The people wouldn't understand. You see how they treat Indians."

"Elias, I would love her like a daughter, and so would your father. Don't you know that?"

"Maybe so, Mother, but it's the people that would be different. And for our children, it wouldn't work."

"You can't go to Canada, Elias. You heard Lieutenant Mosley; it's too dangerous. And it's so far." When Elias did not respond, his mother tried another tack.

"There are a lot of single women marrying-age right here in Lancaster. Haven't you noticed? Mrs. Williams has two daughters, and she was asking about you just the other day. And there are the Millers. And the Jarreds too. You could have your pick."

"You don't understand, Mother. I love Owaissa, and she loves me. She is waiting. I promised." Mrs. Sawyer turned her back and moved to the other side of the kitchen to conceal her emotion. Elias moved to her side and wrapped an arm around her shoulders.

"I don't want to hurt you, Mother, but it's the only way. I can't bring her here. And besides, I liked living with the Indians. People don't understand their way of life. It makes me happy." The kitchen grew silent as Mrs. Sawyer moved out of Elias's grasp and across the room to tend the fire. Elias watched her, his insides turning when she finally spoke.

"You'd better tell your father then. You know this is going to hurt him. He had such high hopes for you."

FORTY-FOUR

T HERE WAS NEW, strange uneasiness whenever Elias's thoughts turned to Owaissa. *What must she have thought when he did not return before the grass grew long as he had promised? Did she look up each time someone pulled back the flap to her lodge, half expecting his smiling face? Did she think he might have been killed? She must be wondering what could have delayed his return. Maybe she would think he did not love her as he had said? If the situation were reversed, how would he have handled it all — not knowing?*

If only he could reach her, to touch her, to assure her he was safe — feeling her breath on his face — waking up next to her after holding her in the quiet of the night as husband and wife. Owaissa would wait, he was sure of that. He had been cruel, but how could he have known how difficult circumstances would have become? There were so many new things that had gotten in the way — the war mainly. And there was something else — he was comfortable. His family was more important than he had realized. This was his home, and he could not deny it was going to be a big step — to leave it all behind.

On the trip south, he had thought about Owaissa, remembering her crying when they said goodbye. She must be worried because she had expected him by now. And Atonwa, he was probably happy he had disappeared. But now Elias's stomach knotted whenever his thoughts turned to Owaissa. There was something else as well — he thought of her less often.

He had planned to leave much sooner, but the summer had moved fast with so much work, and hunting, and church, and visiting relatives and new friends. When he was not busy cutting boards, Elias helped with the season's first hay-cutting and planting the rye field near their garrison house. Then in early June, he had busied himself arranging supplies he would need for the journey, but another week, and then another flew by before July had arrived, and he felt he was ready.

This morning Elias and his father arrived at the mill as usual, hoping to finish the bulk of the day's work early to beat the worst heat of the day. It was a good chance to share his plans, but his father surprised him when he did not understand.

"I know it sounds cruel, Son, but I have to say these things. The Indian girl will move on, just like you will. I am just trying to look out for you."

"I know Father, I know you are. But it's not that simple. I made a promise."

"Sometimes, Elias, we must change our plans — things happen. You have the rest of your life to consider — your nieces and nephews, aunts and uncles. Your family. The business. I planned to turn the mill over to you soon. You're ready now."

Elias was silent as his father's words washed over him.

"I must say this. Consider what's best for everyone. Your home is here, Son. Your mother is failing — you see that, don't you? If you leave now, you may never see her again. Could you turn your back on everyone?"

"I plan to have my own family, Father — with Owaissa. If you knew her, you would not be saying these things. She is special. I only wish I had brought her back with me." Elias was trying to sound resolved, but he was not as sure as he pretended. His father was making sense.

"Elias, listen to me. Owaissa has a family — her people — so do you. People fall in love and marry in an environment. That's why we found so much inter-marriage in the north where Indians and French trappers live together. Like Maurice. It's circumstances." Mr. Sawyer paused while he continued sharpening a saw blade. "But circumstances change, just as yours did. You are back in your world now — things are different. You are trying to fit the past into the present — former experience into now. That's impossible to do." His father must have wondered if his words were working. "Am I making any sense?"

"What if I went back and got her?"

Mr. Sawyer waited for long moments and then spoke, this time in a softer tone.

"Elias, be honest with yourself. If you thought that was possible, you would have done that in the beginning."

Elias snapped, losing some control.

"I'm going back, Father, no matter what you say. Soon too!

And nothing is going to stop me — not you, not the war, not..."

Distant shrieking cut the air, the shrill screams growing louder from the direction of the main village until Sally Hutchins appeared running toward the mill. The hysterical neighbor stumbled to them, her arms flailing above her head until she fell in a pile near the mill door, her shoulders heaving and her hair covering her face.

"Elias! Thomas! Please, please, come quick! They took my girls," she sobbed. "God help me! Please, run. Get them! I beg you!"

Elias's father tried to soothe Sally, but she continued screaming while he struggled to lift her to her feet.

"Tell us. What happened, Sally? Indians?"

"Yes, yes, Thomas! I saw my Ethan shot dead near the barn, and they took Hope and Heather — my baby girls! Oh God, please! Thomas, you have to go after them! Run!"

Elias darted back inside the mill to gather their muskets. After tossing his father his, he ran ahead to the main settlement where he found people already gathering.

"They killed Constance Skillings!" Rebecca Rowlings screamed, flailing her arms then pulling at her hair. "Cut down in the kitchen! I found her there, lying in her blood. And they took my little Martha!"

Elias's father caught up to the group assembling near his house where they learned Jedediah Smith, Peter Williams and his brother Raymond were kidnapped as well.

"We need a rider to go for the militia. Elias, you go, Son!"

"No, Father. We can't wait. I know what their route will be. We must catch them now before they meet up with any others." Elias's gaze met each man. "Who will go with me?"

"I'll go," said Robert Hutchins. Several other men volunteered as well.

"Get extra shot and powder," Elias ordered. "We'll need it when we catch them."

Neighbors rushed home before re-assembling minutes later. The men left immediately, following the Nashua River for two miles before crossing to the northern side, heading northwest where the trail was obvious. It was the same way Elias had traveled after his capture two years ago, and he was confident with luck, they could catch the raiders.

Late morning sun climbed higher in the sky. As the day grew hotter, the men tired quickly. They stopped to rest, then with fatigue slowing them, proceeded more tentatively, watchful, careful not to rush into an ambush. Elias's young legs kept him out front, so late in the afternoon, he was first to find the bodies beside a boulder. Peter Williams lay in blood, his head caved in. Jedidiah lay a few feet away, his skull crushed as well. One of his fingers had been cut off and stuffed into his mouth. The seven men stood frozen.

"Come on," said Elias. "They know we're chasing them; they'll be still running hard. We've got to keep moving." Three hundred rods further, they found four-year-old Martha Rowlings, her dress covered in blood, her head an unrecognizable, bloody stub.

"Lord have mercy," Joshua Prescott groaned with his head shaking as he stood over the child. "The devil himself has been here; this is Satan's work."

Through the rest of the afternoon, the men hurried on, trotting, walking, and then trotting again. When the sun touched the tops of the treetops, they stopped alongside a brook to drink and gather their strength — and courage.

When William Burns spoke, he asked what was on all their minds.

"Do you think they'll kill the rest, Elias?"

"I don't know, William. Maybe not. Only if they slow them down. That's why they killed the others. I pray the two girls are strong enough to keep up." The murder of their neighbors infused the men with a boost of strength and resolve so Elias did not need to coax them when it was time to move again. When it became almost too dark to travel, they stopped.

"We can only rest for a bit," said Elias. "It's been tough moving, I know. But if we can keep going, this will be our best chance to catch them. They won't think we will travel at night. We might have enough moonlight to see, as long as we have the river to follow. If we do not keep going, they will lose us by tomorrow, and the girls will be gone. They will probably feel safe enough to stop for a few hours, and we can close the gap. It's our only chance."

When they were ready to go, Elias cautioned the men with a whisper.

"Stay quiet now. No talking. And be careful; they will have a rearguard watching for followers. There is no telling when we might come upon them."

The men trotted in silence through the night. The mosquitoes patted their faces and necks, but the air was cooler, and they maintained a steady pace until the sky began to turn dawn-pink over the eastern horizon. Elias led them north, peeling their group away from the river near a ridge he recognized.

"It's this way," he motioned. "I remember this place."

They climbed an easy slope toward the top of an exposed ridge where the underbrush grew thin, and the view to the top was less interrupted by trees. Ezekiel Stebbins moved near Elias's side as they entered a slight clearing.

"Bang!" The bark of a musket broke the dawn quiet, and as the men dove to the ground, Ezekiel crumbled next to Elias with blood bubbling from a red bullet hole near the center of his forehead. The higher ground above them erupted in a flurry of sound and smoke as Elias and the five men scrambled to find cover and return fire. The fight continued with musket balls slapping the trees and the air clouding with thick white smoke and the smell of burning powder.

When a lull came, Elias heard a familiar voice yell above an occasional musket shot.

"Elias, it's me! Do not shoot, Elias! It is your friend, Joachim!"

One by one, all the muskets stopped firing until the woods were completely still.

"Elias, I am here — with Wematin and Rowi — Awasos too. We are all here — with Atonwa! There are many of us — with many weapons. We have joined the rest of our party. It is bad for you. Go back or you will all die."

The men were spread hiding behind logs and trees but close enough for Elias to feel their eyes watching him, waiting for his lead.

"You know these devils?" shouted William from the base of a tree yards away. Elias ignored the question.

"Joachim, I curse you!" he screamed while struggling to understand. "You've come to my home? Has Satan captured your heart?"

Elias rose in a crouch to fire at the movement he thought might be Joachim. Muskets on both sides erupted again with gunpowder smoke filling the space between opponents. Peter Jacobs, who had crouched behind a thick oak tree, screamed and jerked in spasm when a ball slammed into his neck. He fell backward, groaning while writhing on the ground until he was finally quiet and still. Musket balls slapped the leaves overhead while Elias stayed flattened behind a fallen log to reload. Pieces of bark split, showering from the tree trunks near his head as the barrage of shots continued. When the flurry finally quieted enough, Elias yelled again.

"Joachim, we just want the prisoners. Let them go, and no one else will need to die. The militia will be here soon. Then they will kill you all!"

The woods remained still. Elias hoped more men were really coming, and feared if the Indians attacked, rushed them in a wave, the soldiers would find them all dead. Joachim broke the quiet.

"Elias! Atonwa wants to parley. But only you, he say."

"Don't trust those snakes!" someone shouted. "They will cut you down!" After more quiet, Joachim yelled again.

"Elias, trust me. Atonwa, he say he will come unarmed. You do the same. Tell your men. Please, mon ami. It is your only way. You cannot win. We will attack and kill you all, but first parley. Atonwa wants to talk."

"Don't fall for that, Elias," yelled William.

"It's a trick," another man yelled. "You can't trust them."

"Maybe," answered Elias. "I do know him; he's a devil for sure, but we have no choice. Who has a knife?" When Ralph Ferguson tossed over a hunting knife, Elias slid it into his boot and pulled his trouser leg over it. The men were all quiet, watching Elias's for his next move. "I don't trust him, and if he does what I am suspecting, at least it will be a fair fight. If I win, they'll run but maybe spare the girls." Elias's next comment was made as he stood and moved away from the tree. "If not...maybe you can hold them off until the militia catches up. All right, Atonwa," he yelled. "I'm coming out. No tricks!"

When Elias walked a few steps, Atonwa showed himself as well, his wide form easing from behind a large pine tree. The two men moved across the clearing, covering the ground quickly, with Elias responding in kind, mimicking Atonwa's quick, confident strut. When they were almost close enough to touch, they stopped. Atonwa looked heavier, but his appearance had not changed much. He wore only a breechcloth and leggings, his chest bare, his face blackened with dye covering all but his eyes. Both men stared as if measuring each other's resolve. When Atonwa spoke, his words were part Abenaki, English and French.

"English. You die today. You see I have many — too many for you. You want to live? You go now."

Elias responded in Abenaki as if to show Atonwa he was not intimidated.

"No, Atonwa. Return the captives, then we let you go. Or you die."

The conversation stalled, and Atonwa showed a slight smile as if the meeting were ending. Elias was wary, expecting a sudden move from Atonwa until the brave continued in a surprisingly quieter, even tone.

"You know our ways, English. The girls are why we come. I cannot release; the others will see this."

Elias sensed hesitation in Atonwa's demeanor he had never seen before.

"We plan to fight, Atonwa, until our militia arrives. If you run, we will follow and leave the trail for our soldiers."

Atonwa released a mocking laugh.

"Your soldiers are far away. Your English, the three men, they are dead. If you fight more, maybe we kill girls too — before soldiers can come. And we kill you."

Elias did not answer while he considered his response. Atonwa cast a glance back toward the woods where his men watched, then returned his full attention to Elias, speaking in a more subdued, almost confidential tone.

"You lie, English. Men no come soon. You know, I know. You brave but much alone — and a fool. You see my men; they are many."

Atonwa was right. Elias did not argue but waited, trying to discern the brave's real motive for the talking. After another almost nervous glance backward, Atonwa offered his solution.

"I give girls, English. You swear."

"That's fine, Atonwa. That's all we want."

"No," said Atonwa, his voice approaching a rough whisper. "You make true oath. You go back. Stay. Never come again my land."

Elias tried to absorb what Atonwa's words had meant — the girls' release, unharmed — if he promised not to return to Canada. Hope and Heather would go back to their families. It was almost too easy. He would not have to honor a promise to stay out of Canada. What would it matter? Who would know? His family and friends would understand. But then Atonwa's bargain began to become clearer. Things were different with the Abenaki. Atonwa would use his broken word to shame him in front of the People — and Owaissa. He could never live with that.

Joachim and Lazar had been right — about Atonwa. He was indeed a great warrior. He had won, and now Elias had only one choice.

"All right, Atonwa. You win. Release the girls."

"English oath? English has true heart?"

"I do," said Elias. "I do. I swear it. I will not go back to Canada."

Atonwa measured Elias for long moments while they stood close, their faces almost touching.

"You make good fight, English. Now we see if you make a good oath … true like Abenaki do."

Atonwa wheeled and strode back across the clearing before disappearing into the woods. Elias eased back to his cover as well and waited. After a few minutes, Joachim appeared from the edge of the trees, holding the hands of the seven-year-old girl and her eight-year-old sister. He stopped halfway across the clearing, and when he had released the girls, Hope and Heather ran the rest of the way, crying with their long brown hair flowing out behind. Joachim stood in the middle of the clearing.

Elias almost yelled; there was much he might have said. But instead, he just returned Joachim's stare until the brave lifted and held his arms waist high with palms up, then dropped them and turned away.

They carried the bodies of Raymond Williams and Ezekiel until approaching the place they had found the first victims. Soon after, Lieutenant Mosley and twenty mounted militia caught up to them and dispatched men to help them return to Lancaster.

******

ON THE WAY home, Elias had time to think about a lot of things — Canada and Lancaster — his family — Owaissa and himself. At home he joined his neighbors sharing their unbridled celebration and thanksgiving for the rescued girls along with intense grief for the murdered. The dead were buried, and people began to return to their necessary activities, improving defenses, harvesting crops, leaving their sadness behind to embrace the chore of staying alive.

On the first day of September, Reverend Prentice surprised the hushed congregation assembled in the meetinghouse with a letter from Boston.

"'Two days ago, at dawn, a war party of natives — close to one hundred, I am told, including French militia, fell on the settlement of Haverhill, killing sixteen of our people — men, women and children — some in their fields, others inside their garrisons. Michael White was cut down along with his young son as he worked in his field.

Most of the houses were burned, along with the meeting house. I do not have to remind you this is the second such assault on Haverhill. Thank God they were much more prepared, or the massacre could have been even worse. A few women were able to save their families. Mrs. Swan grabbed her cooking spit from the fire and drove the hot metal through the belly of a savage. The town had not enough coffins, and instead, a large pit was dug in the burial ground for the sixteen dead.

The attackers had many guns, and their rearguard was able to prevent our men from catching up to the main group. But due to the heroism of our brave neighbors, nine attackers were killed, and some of the captives were freed, but the savages escaped with over twenty of our people. I am sorry to say we fear they may be lost to us. Houses were burning, and the watchhouse was torn apart as the attack continued.'"

The service ended with much murmuring and sobbing with Reverend Prentice so weakened he had difficulty finishing. Finally the people oozed out of the meetinghouse in a stunned shuffle. As the next few days passed, Elias found himself avoiding the eyes of others, as if he could be judged for knowing the attackers. His feelings began to become more clear, and he knew.

"I've decided, Father. I can't go back. Not now. Not after all that has happened." His father did not respond, as if he knew Elias had more to say. "We are just too different — Owaissa and me, I mean — our two worlds are too different. There is too much in between. You were right — about circumstances. The life I made in Canada I will have to leave there. I can see now this is where I belong."

Elias's father offered no additional comment, allowing the matter to complete. Elias moved away, feeling thankful he did not have to tell everything — about his oath. The dream had been that — only a dream, and now it was gone. *If only he had gone back to Canada as he had planned, he and Owaissa might have lived the life they had imagined.* Now he would trust his faith in Providence and do what he knew he must. He would try to ignore his fear it might never be finished and would pray Owaissa's God would help her move on quickly; it was for the best. Most of all, he would pray to his own God as well — for the strength to face the regret that might someday surely come for him.

THE END

"Elias Sawyer returned to Lancaster,
bringing wonderful gifts."

"On his deathbed, Elias is reported to have expressed regret he
did not return to Owaissa as he'd promised."

Lancaster Historian, John Smith
History of Lancaster: 1870

AFTERWORD

Two years later, in 1710, Elias and Beatrix Houghton married. Elias was twenty-one, Beatrix twenty-four. Elias's father, at sixty-one, turned over the operation of the mill to Elias, and over the next several years, while the Sawyer business prospered, Beatrix delivered five children: Elijah, Thankful, Elisha, Betty and Prudence.

When Elias's mother, Hannah, died in 1718 at sixty-nine, Elias's father married his third wife, the widow, Mary White. Mary died in August 1733, and Thomas married his fourth wife, Anna Ross, on December 15, the same year. Three years later, in 1736, Thomas passed on at the age of eighty-seven.

Elias lived to the age of sixty-three and died in 1752. His body is buried in the Old Common Burial Ground across from the third Lancaster meeting house that stood on Wilder Road. His father, Thomas, and grandfather, the original Thomas Sawyer, along with other first settlers' remains, including Lancaster's founder, John Prescott, lie nearby in the Original Settlers Graveyard. It's hidden in the woods behind the first meetinghouse location, each grave marked with only a rough fieldstone.

After Elias's death, beginning in 1763 and continuing for the next seven years, New England continued to be embroiled in the French and Indian War, the last imperial confrontation between England and France for control of the North American continent. The conflict's outcome was determined with the blood of New England Colonial Militiamen, French soldiers and the native people of the land surrounding what is known today as the St. Lawrence Seaway.

The Sawyer family continued in the mill business; one of Elias's grandsons, also named Elias, built another sawmill in the town of Templeton. A French survey reported that by the end of Elias's life, over thirteen mills had been built in Canada, all constructed using what the French described as "the English colonists' design."

Sawyer descendants number in the tens of thousands, scattered throughout America, all traced back to the original pioneer who sailed from England in 1643 and helped establish a settlement they called Nashaway — a tiny community at the meeting of the waters of the north and south branches of the Nashua River.

Owaissa's earthen plate remained in the Sawyer family for several generations until Sarah Sawyer, a last remaining widow, bequeathed it to the Thayer Memorial Library in the Sawyers' home of Lancaster, Massachusetts. Curious twenty-first-century viewers can find the plate on display and perhaps wonder about the hands that made it and Elias Sawyer's regret.

THE SAWYER FAMILY

<u>Thomas Sawyer</u>: 1615 – 1706

- Original Sawyer from Lincolnshire, England who arrived in the Massachusetts Bay Colony in 1636 at the age of twenty.
- Migrated to Rowley near the Atlantic coast in 1643 and then on to the Nashaway Plantation in 1646.
- Married Sarah Prescott, the daughter of John Prescott, one of the four founders of Nashaway at the meeting of the north and south branches of the Nashua River.
- Thomas Sawyer, (Elias's grandfather), died September 1706, at ninety-one.

<u>Thomas Sawyer, (Elias's father)</u>: 1649 – 1736

- Born in Lancaster, 1649, the first of fourteen children.
- At twenty-one, Thomas married twenty-five-year-old, Sarah Fairbanks, August 11, 1670. Sarah died sixteen months later, January 2, 1672.
- Thomas married twenty-three-year-old Hannah Lewis, September 21, 1672.
- Seven years later, Hannah gave birth to Hannah, followed by William, Joseph, Bezaleel, and finally, in 1689, Elias Sawyer.
- When Hannah died, July 15, 1718, Thomas, at sixty-nine, married the sixty-two-year-old widow, Mary Rice White who died August 22, 1733.

- Thomas married Anna Ross on December 15, 1733, who outlived Thomas before her death in 1753 at age fifty-four.
- Thomas died in 1736 at age eighty-seven.

Elias Sawyer: 1689 – 1752

- In 1710, at twenty-one, Elias married Beatrix Houghton. Beatrix was twenty-four.
- Beatrix's first children were twins, Elijah and Elisha, who died in the same year of their birth.
- Other children included Betty, in 1712, followed by Elijah, (1713), Thankful, (1715), Elisha in 1718 and finally Prudence in 1726.
- Elias died in 1752, at sixty-three, followed by his wife, Beatrix eighteen years later in 1770 at age eighty-five.

Elisha Sawyer's Children

- Elisha's children included Elisha, born in 1744, Jotham, born in 1745 and the youngest brother Elias, born 1747 who built his own sawmill in Templeton, MA.

HISTORICAL NOTES

- The Sawyers and John Bigelow were captured October 15th in 1705, the third year of the conflict later labeled Queen Anne's war that saw England, France and Spain fighting, not only in Europe, but on the North American Continent. Many consider the contest the First World War.

- All told, the inhabitants of Deerfield lost forty-four dead — ten men, nine women, twenty-five children. Five of the garrison militia and nine Hadley militiamen were also killed. The raiders also suffered casualties, reported somewhere between eleven and forty killed with twenty-two wounded. In addition, one-hundred-nine inhabitants of Deerfield were taken captive and marched to Canada. On the journey north, several captives died of starvation, or exposure or were killed by the Indians; eighty-nine reached Canada alive.

- While Elias, Thomas and John worked in Canada, the first newspaper was launched in Boston, and a family named Franklin christened their thirteenth infant son, Benjamin.

- It would be another thirty years before later, well-known heroes Paul Revere and Thomas Jefferson were born.

- Elias died in 1752, at age sixty-three.

- Two years after Elias's death, a twenty-year-old lieutenant named George Washington instigated a fight with a French and Indian scouting party in the wilderness that later became Pennsylvania. News of the incident moved slowly but finally escalated throughout Europe to become the flashpoint of the French and Indian War — the final colonial contest for the North American continent.

- September 13, 1759, the Battle of Quebec, Bataille Des Plaines d'Abraham, was the culmination of a three-month siege by the British. The final battle lasted fifteen minutes.
- On September 8, 1760, Governor General Pierre, Marquis de Vaudreuil-Cavagnal, surrendered the entire French colony known as Canada to the British, and with the Treaty of Paris in 1763 New France was officially ceded to Britain.
- The Treaty of Paris made the northern portion of New France, (including Canada and some additional lands to the south and west), officially a British colony.
- A year after John's return, the Bigelow's fifth child, Comfort, was born. In the following years, John's wife Jerusha delivered eight more children.
- Jerusha died in Marlborough in 1758 at age eighty-one.
- John died in Marlborough as well, eleven years later, at age ninety-four.
- The captives stayed a year to build the mill on the Chambly River, the first in France's new world of Canada. By 1719, nineteen sawmills had been built in Canada, made, in the words of the French, "in the English design."
- Over the years, the original area of the Nashaway settlement, later called Lancaster, was gradually segmented into the towns of Lancaster, Harvard, Clinton, Bolton, Leominster, Berlin and Sterling, along with parts of West Boylston.
- The Nashua River still slides through Lancaster, Massachusetts, remaining much the same as during the Sawyers' capture over three hundred years ago.

AUTHOR'S NOTE

This work was inspired by reading the inscription etched on the old, three-foot, granite marker tilted in the high spring grass near the side of the road in Lancaster, Massachusetts.

"On this spot on October 15, 1705, the Indians captured John Bigelow, Thomas Sawyer and his son, Elias and carried them to Canada."

When I'd read the words, my eyes lifted and wandered across the meadow to the pond beyond, trying to imagine what had happened here long ago. I wondered what was going on in the world three hundred years ago to compel raiders to make the long, dangerous walk from Canada to kidnap these men. Most importantly, as my imagination raced, I wanted to learn how old was Elias and what might the fear and that adventure have been like for a young person. And as I did, I decided that I wanted to tell his story.

Owaissa's Earthen Plate

Stored at Thayer Memorial Library,
Lancaster, Massachusetts

SPECIAL THANKS

Special thanks for assistance in bringing this book to life goes to my wife Linda for detailed editing, Ann Frantz and Hollis Shore with Seven Bridge Writers' Collaborative Critique Groups, Laraine Armenti for assistance in cover design and text, Maria Day, Joyce Derenas and Kathy Haaker for editorial assistance, Marcia Jakubowicz with Thayer Memorial Library Special Historical Collection assistance, Rich Marcello for assistance with story structure, Pat Campbell, Conant Public Library Director, for inviting me to host a National Novel Writers' Month seminar, (NaNoWriMo), during which this work was begun, and Jane Boudrot for her continued encouragement and support.

ADDITIONAL WORK by
E. RAYMOND TATTEN

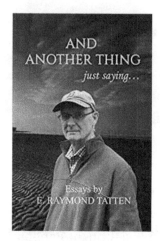

AND ANOTHER THING.....
just saying

In this, his first collection, *AND ANOTHER THING, just saying...*, E. Raymond Tatten offers thirty-five essays, short bursts in response to bubbled-up memories and current events.

What readers say:

- *The best reading is when someone writes the book you wish you had written.*
- *35 short stories/essays about everyday topics that the author turns into extraordinary tales with the magic of his words. Raymond Tatten is a pure storyteller.*
- *This book draws the reader through a variety of emotions and brings all the "memoirs" we have inside of us to the surface. The writing is artful, which makes for an easy and entertaining read. If you like memoir-style books this should certainly be on your "to read" list.*
- *An eclectic compilation of memories, advice and wonderment. These essays are short but possess enough "meat" to keep one's mind nourished, even after you've walked away from the book. Through his writing, the author reveals much of who he is and the road he traveled to get there.*

TEX MOSTLY

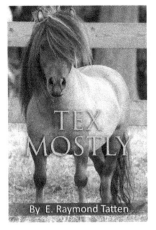

Tex Mostly is the author's story as a nine-year-old who is transplanted from a city apartment to live for the first time at his father's remote farm hidden in the thick woods of Central Massachusetts.

The acclaimed short story portrays unexpected excitement found on the farm during a summer afternoon along with events that force a boy to mature faster than he would have liked.

Short-listed for "Short Story of the Year" by *Adelaide Literary Magazine*

Print Book and e-book Available on AMAZON

Author Reading available on EDWARD TATTEN YOUTUBE
youtube.com/channel/UCrh4FAAfUCcBZ0DcNSEjQ9A

MOVING WILLIE

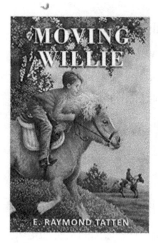

AMAZON REVIEW: 5 STARS
"It's all just one emotion after another, worded in such an evocative tone. What a great read…"

Moving Willie is a story set in 1957 where worlds intersect — the city and the farm, the future and the past, the boy and adult when nine-year-old Willie Tatten meets surprising challenges bigger and more important than a boy might have imagined.

******

"I scuffed my boots across the gravel yard, hoping the day had made everything all right. The barn door was open the quarter way it always was. It never closed all the way. I pushed, letting what was left of late afternoon sunshine spill in over my shoulders, awakening the barn's insides.

'Tex?'"

******

"Strange high-pitched whines leaked from a few of the pigs, as they seemed unsure of their safety for the first time since coming to the pen. It was strange how the animals had sensed trouble, and the sounds they made were as if they had started to cry."

PRINT & E-BOOK AVAILABLE ON AMAZON

ABOUT THE AUTHOR

E. Raymond Tatten is a life-long Yankee living in the beautiful apple country of Central Massachusetts. His essays and articles have appeared in many local publications, and some selected works can be heard on his YouTube channel, Edward Tatten YouTube.

Tatten shares a home on Rowley Hill, Sterling, Massachusetts with his wife Linda, daughter KT and a five-pound female Yorkie named Dani Dog.

E. RAYMOND TATTEN CONTACT INFORMATION:

Facebook: E. Raymond Tatten Author Page

E-mail: ramun55@comcast.net

Webpage: eraymondtatten.com

LinkedIn: Raymond Tatten

Edward Tatten YouTube:

youtube.com/channel/UCrh4FAAfUCcBZ0DcNSEjQ9A

Printed in the USA
CPSIA information can be obtained
at www.ICGtesting.com
LVHW092153211123
764606LV00040B/302